A Prayer to No God

The Void

"She had begged for a god, so he became one."

A Prayer to No God

The Godless World
Book 1

Nicole A. Sterling

Content Warnings

This novel contains dark, intense, and psychologically charged themes that may be disturbing to some readers.

A Prayer to No God explores devotion, betrayal, faith, and power through a dark monster romance lens. It is a story about what happens when belief breaks and what answers in the silence.

Please proceed with care and prioritize your well-being. Themes and content include:

Graphic violence and gore

On-page murder

Body horror and supernatural distortion

Religious trauma and deconstruction of faith

Familial betrayal and emotional abandonment

Misogyny and the commodification of women

Psychological intensity and isolation

Possessive, obsessive romantic dynamics

Power imbalance between a human and an immortal being

Themes of ownership and devotion

Explicit sexual content

References to coercion and forced marriage

This story contains morally gray characters and explores unhealthy dynamics that evolve into chosen devotion.

Your mental health matters.

This world is dark, but the romance is fluffy.

Enjoy!

Contents

Prologue

Lyssena loved to sit beneath her favorite tree.

There was only one like it. It was just past the edge of the fields where the grass grew tall and golden, and the air always smelled like sun-warmed soil and something green. The tree bent slightly to one side, its branches reaching out as if trying to hold the sky. Beneath its shade, the world grew softer. Not many people ever came there. It wasn't a place for chores or errands, and it stood too far from the path to be convenient. So, it became hers.

In that quiet patch of earth, Lyssena could simply be.

She didn't have to speak, kneel, or make herself smaller. She didn't have to listen to rules or carry baskets or pray beneath anyone's watchful eye. Alone, there was no one to impress, no one to disappoint. She could stretch her legs out in the dirt, trace circles in the dust with her fingers, and hum to herself without worrying if her voice was proper.

There was no need to bow when no one stood above her.

To Lyssena, it was as simple as that. You don't make yourself smaller for someone who isn't there.

She learned that early. Not from pain exactly, but from presence. Or the lack of it.

Often, little Lyssena would find herself alone for reasons she didn't always understand. Her five brothers were loud and full of movement, always together, always pushing and pulling, wrestling and teasing each other with the kind of rough affection boys were allowed to show. They had their own orbit, and she wasn't part of it.

When she wasn't cooking or mending, her mother was always near Father. She existed in the quiet space between his words and moods, holding things together. There was love there, Lyssena could see that. But it was a love that left little room for her to step into.

So Lyssena learned to love her own company.

She would walk the village paths at odd hours, pick flowers she'd never name, and arrange stones in patterns only she would see. She knew how to braid her hair without help, how to patch a hem in silence, and how to swallow questions she didn't know who to ask.

She was never hungry. Her father made sure of that. She never went without shoes or shawls or sweets when the festival came. Her family loved her—of this, she was certain—but it was the kind of love that sometimes felt like looking at a warm house from outside the window. You could see it glowing. You knew it was there. But you weren't always invited inside.

Still. . . she was happy.

Not the kind of happiness that bursts out in laughter or dances around a fire, but a quieter thing. A soft, enduring contentment that lived in small rituals of the day: the way her father ruffled her hair when she passed him, the rare times her brothers invited her to watch them spar or play in the new cave they found, and the way her mother gently combed her hair before bed, even when distracted. These were not grand gestures. But they were enough to convince a little girl that she was wanted, even if not always understood.

A family of eight, all appearing happy, would have seemed like a lie if you weren't wealthy—and they were not.

They had meat, but not often. They had coin, but not enough to waste. Her dresses were worn, but mended. The blankets were thin, but warm. There was love, but sometimes it was tired.

Still, Lyssena grew up believing she was loved. For a child, that was enough.

Maybe that's why the betrayal hurt the way it did: not like a strike on the face, but like a soft erasure.

Because love that teaches you how to be alone is not the kind that teaches you how to be safe.

Chapter One

Milk and Honey

Lyssena

There were five gods they prayed to.

Kalos, god of harvest. Jenar, god of health. Syvaar, god of life. Leyeer, god of wealth. There was another god, though his name was unknown to men, and therefore unknown to Lyssena. At twenty-three she knew he existed, just like everyone did, but that was where it ended.

Now, with her knees bent and palms pressed gently before her chest, Lyssena prayed.

Oh, greatest Kalos, I beg you to hear my plea.

I vow to kneel and obey, to bow my head and honor the land I asked you to bless.

Oh, greatest Kalos, my words are nothing before your greatness, and yet I beg. I pray.

Lyssena's family always said that because she had green eyes, her prayers belonged to Kalos. Her brothers, born with brown eyes, prayed to Leyeer.

Jenar and Syvaar were part of their morning rituals. Those gods did not seem to mind the color of one's gaze.

Greatest Syvaar, I wanted to ask you to watch for me tonight. I was afraid to face your greatness at the morning prayer with my people. Now that I'm alone with your grace and knowledge, I shall say at once what lies on my heart. Greatest Syvaar, let tonight's meeting go well. I hope I find this man just fine. Oh, greatest Syvaar; please, I beg you.

Help me have a better life.

She bowed her head before the dark entrance of a sacred room no one was ever meant to enter, then rose slowly to her feet.

The seeds had been planted, offerings laid, words spoken, and prayers whispered. She had asked for the crops to grow.

In that quiet moment, Lyssena felt content. Not joyful exactly, but full.

This was the task of the sinful: to pray and beg for forgiveness until the day the skies welcomed them. It was also the task of the sinful to ask for kindness from gods who owed them nothing.

But today was different. Today was a sacred day.

And tonight. . . tonight she would be engaged.

"Lyssena, dearest, have you prayed again?"

She turned at the sound of a soft, familiar voice. The temple leader stood in the hallway, robed in white, as leader after leader maintained the same tradition.

Lyssena lowered her gaze. It was not proper for an unmarried woman to meet the eyes of a man. She could look at her father, of course, and her brothers, but other men were forbidden. Not unless she was given permission.

"Yes," she murmured, a small smile pulling at her lips. "I have asked the great Kalos for a good harvest."

To lie was to sin. But she had not lied; therefore, she had

not sinned. She simply hadn't told everything. That was fine, so long as she hadn't spoken something untrue.

The thud of leather shoes echoed off the stone walls, each step landing like a soft commandment in the hush of the temple.

A shadow stretched across the floor tiles, long and angular in the fractured afternoon light that spilled through stained-glass windows.

"A good harvest is important, isn't it?" the leader asked.

"It is."

"Go now. You have much to prepare for, Lyssena."

She nodded quickly. The fine linen of her shawl brushed her neck as she rose. Her gaze remained lowered, fixed on the mosaic-patterned floors beneath her feet. She hurried toward the great temple doors, the tall, massive things carved from dark wood.

"Have a good day, Lyssena," the temple keeper called behind her, his voice echoing in the vastness of the holy place.

"Thank you, keeper," she murmured and opened one of the doors.

Outside, the air was warm and fragrant, and she smelled dust and wildflowers. She didn't lift her eyes, but her feet knew the path. Once, as a child, she would trip over every stone and root. Now she walked with confidence, even with her head bowed. It was easier that way. You were less likely to fall when you crossed the same path so many times.

The sun hung high, warming the top of her covered head. Around her, the village lived and breathed.

A blacksmith's hammer rang out, and she matched her steps to its rhythm. Somewhere down the road, a goat bleated, followed by the gentler sound of cows behind a wooden fence. Children shrieked with laughter, darting between thatched cottages.

A cart rolled past, one wheel bumping against stone. The creak of wood echoed in protest beneath the weight it carried. Near the well, two women spoke in hushed voices. Lyssena caught her name, then silence. The wind lifted the edge of her shawl, and laundry flapped like flags beside them.

"I heard he's a knight!"

"Oh, perhaps a big dowry was paid."

"Yes, yes. Poor Lyssena."

"Shut it—"

Everyone knew that today Lyssena would meet her knight.

Gods, she hoped he was a good man. She wished for a happy life and to be a happy wife.

Bees hummed in the wildflowers that edged the road, and somewhere nearby, a dog barked. Once, then again. The air carried a medley of smells: baking bread, smoke, sweat, and the sweet tang of ripe fruit. It was an ordinary day for everyone else but Lyssena.

As she neared her home, Lyssena finally lifted her gaze. She rushed past the garden, past the fat pigs snorting near the fence, and past the gate where vines curled like lazy fingers. Her mother stood by the open door, brushing flour from her dress, leaving pale streaks in scattered patterns across the fabric.

"Come, Lyssena, come!" her mother urged, already turning to lead her inside.

Lyssena followed, and the door closed softly behind them.

"Have you prayed for tonight?" her mother asked.

Lyssena nodded and reached up to remove the scarf from her head. "I did. And I was careful."

"Did anyone notice?"

"The leader and the keeper, Mother. But no one else."

She folded the scarf and held it out. Her mother took it

with distracted fingers, her gaze flicking along Lyssena's sides, never quite settling on her face.

"Don't worry," Lyssena added gently. "I haven't lied."

"What did you say?"

"I prayed for a good harvest."

"It wasn't a lie?"

"It wasn't. I truly did pray for that."

Her mother exhaled slowly, the tension easing from her shoulders.

"Your father said he's a good man," she said at last, clutching the folded scarf in both hands. "Yes. A very good man. I know we did well."

She nodded, more to herself than to Lyssena, and there was something in the gesture that felt strange. Not unkind.

Just. . . odd.

The next few hours passed quickly.

Her father and brothers were out hunting while Lyssena remained home with her mother, preparing to welcome the man who would soon be her husband.

Most girls were married much younger than she was—at sixteen, mostly—but her father had waited. He wanted to secure their future properly, and with Lyssena's green eyes and pretty face, that had been more than possible. This knight, Kaan, she had heard his name was, had been at war for many years. He had given their people a name to be proud of. He had coin, land, and reputation. Lyssena was afraid, but not too much. She knew her father would never lie.

"You have such lush waves, dear," her mother murmured, coughing softly as she drew the comb gently through Lyssena's hair. "I used to have that kind of hair when I was young. Your father once held it in his palm and said our children would have the same. And he was right."

Lyssena smiled at her reflection in the mirror, its wooden frame carved with curling vines. She loved that mirror. Its frame was as light as her hair.

Lyssena and her mother sat in her room—hers alone—while her brothers shared the larger room across the hall. She had always been her parents' little princess. In this quiet moment, she felt it more than ever.

Her hair fell in soft waves down her back, the color of fresh-cut wheat. Most summers, the sun would have kissed her skin with freckles across her nose and cheeks. But this year, she hadn't worked the fields. This summer had been set aside. Reserved for preparing.

For meeting her knight.

"Do you think the knight is kind?" Lyssena asked, pulling the brushed half of her hair over one shoulder as her mother began working through the rest.

The room was quiet, save for the soft scratch of the comb and the faint crackle of a few lit candles. Her mother had already scrubbed her back until it gleamed. *Glowing,* she had called it. Lyssena must look her best for tonight.

"He is, yes," her mother said at last. "A kind man. Just. . . hardened from war."

She spoke slowly. There was a pause after the words, a small silence that made Lyssena wonder if her mother was nervous too. Perhaps she was praying, just as Lyssena had, that everything would be alright.

Lyssena believed it would be. It *had* to be.

Her mother had been feeding her more than usual over the past few months. Rich stews, honeyed bread, dried fruits soaked in sweet wine. She had gained just enough weight to appear fuller and more plump. In their village, softness was seen as a sign of health, of care for a daughter well-loved by her family.

It was a kind of love expressed in roasted meat and second helpings, and the way her father smiled and teased her into finishing every bite.

He had even brought her fabric for a new dress, though they had little to spare. Her mother had added rose oil to the bathwater that evening. For weeks now, Lyssena had soaked her hands in honey and milk. Luxuries they did not often afford.

She was grateful, deeply so. As she was getting so much attention.

And she could hardly wait to meet him.

Chapter Two

The Fifth Flame

Lyssena

Lyssena stood still, her hands resting at her sides, as her mother finished tying the white gown at her back. The fabric was soft and weightless, finer than anything she had ever worn. Her hair, freshly combed and still damp from her bath, tumbled in loose waves down to the small of her back.

Her mother stepped in front of her and carefully placed a white, silky hairpiece at the crown of Lyssena's head. It draped like moonlight, pinned in place with a simple mother-of-pearl clip—an heirloom, once hers.

"There," her mother whispered. "You look just like I did the night I was chosen by your father."

Before Lyssena could answer, the sound of boots striking earth reached them. Voices calling, a bark of laughter carried in from the outside.

"They're back," she breathed, her heart leaping. Without waiting for permission, she gathered up her skirts and ran barefoot toward the front door.

The sunlight stung her eyes for a moment, but then she saw her father and all five of her brothers, just now returning from the hunt.

Her eldest brothers, Koren and Damyn, led the group. Broad-shouldered and grinning, each had a string of rabbits tied to their belts, the animals swinging with every step, ears bobbing like small pendulums. Between them and their father, they carried a large deer, each man gripping a leg as they hauled the animal together. Its head and chest dragged in the dirt, the fur along its flank stained dark with blood.

At the threshold, her three younger brothers—Hale, Renn, and Vos—were doubled over, panting hard as if they had hauled the rest of the deer's weight from the carriage to the house. Now they leaned on their knees, sweat on their brows, faces flushed but grinning ear to ear.

"Lyssena!" Hale called, his voice cracking with joy and exertion. "We brought back the biggest one!"

"All for you!" Damyn shouted, lifting his string of rabbits in triumph.

She laughed and rushed forward, throwing her arms around her father just as he dropped the deer at the edge of the step. He smelled of pine, sweat, and blood. His arms, rough and strong, were supposed to wrap around her like they always had, but this time, he pulled back to look at her.

"You're ready," he said, stepping half a pace away.

His eyes softened as he took in the sight of her in white. "You. . . beautiful."

Lyssena flushed but smiled. "Mother made me lovely," she whispered.

"No," her father said, pressing a kiss to her forehead after wiping the sweat over his brow onto his sleeve. "We just helped you shine."

The boys gathered around them, voices overlapping,

teasing and boasting about who had hunted what. Lyssena stood among them, heart full.

"Let me help with preparing! There's so much food," she offered.

But Father shook his head. "You are clean and ready. I'll skin the game, and your brothers will help." He turned to her mother then. "Dear, will you cook it for us?"

Both Lyssena and her father looked to her. Her mother nodded.

As the sound of voices and laughter echoed from the main room where the men worked, Lyssena slipped away. Her room, calmer and quieter, welcomed her. The light had begun to shift, afternoon leaning into evening, and golden beams poured through the window, softening the edges of the day.

She closed the door behind her and crossed to the small table by the window. The shutters were open, and a breeze moved gently through the space, stirring the edges of a folded cloth on the dresser.

She knelt.

Beside the window sat five candles, arranged in an arc. She always kept them there—five flames for five gods. Five slender pillars of wax, all used except for one. The fifth remained whole. Always whole.

She struck the flint and lit the first.

"Oh, greatest Kalos," she whispered, watching the wick catch and bloom into light. "Grant us strong crops and full baskets. Let the deer be fed well so their meat is rich. Let our trees bear fruit without rot."

The second candle flared with a soft pop. "Greatest Leyeer, let this home remain rich. Not only in coin, but in peace. Let no hunger or bitterness touch us this season."

Then the third. "Jenar, keeper of bones and breath, let my

father's hands not ache, let my brothers heal quickly, let none of us grow sick in the cold months to come."

And the fourth. "Syvaar. Oh, Syvaar," she whispered more gently. "Tonight, I ask something small and foolish: let him smile at me. Let my voice not fail. Let my words be sweet and my laugh light. Give me courage. And a little beauty, if you will."

The flame danced on the fourth wick, painting a warm glow across Lyssena's knuckles. Her eyes drifted then, slowly, to the fifth candle.

She reached for the flint again, her fingers brushing its edge, but she didn't strike it.

No one prayed to this god.

There was no name for it in their books. No statue in the temple. Only the fifth flame, kept out of habit—or perhaps out of fear—for something they had never dared to name.

She didn't know what it governed. Didn't know if it listened. But it had always been there, a shadow among the light.

She wondered, just for a moment, what might happen if she lit it. Suppose she whispered into the space where a name should be. Suppose she asked for something she should never want.

But she didn't.

She let the silence wrap around her like a veil and bowed her head before four flickering flames and one quiet sentinel.

Lyssena hadn't spoken much to men before. A few polite exchanges with the temple leader and the keeper, of course.

Oh, and that one man at the market who had sold them pears. He'd had a kind voice, she thought. Or maybe that had been the man with the onions?

She didn't remember their faces, only vague echoes of words that barely counted as conversation.

She was comfortable with her father and brothers, but that was different. They were hers. They didn't count as *men* in the way this knight would. A stranger. A husband.

How was she supposed to speak to a man she didn't know?

She turned to the mirror once more and tried again.

"Hello, my name is Lyssena," she said aloud. Immediately, she winced. *He already knows my name,* she thought. That was foolish. Why would she say it like he'd never heard it before? What if he thought she assumed he'd forgotten? That might seem rude. Would it?

She sighed and pressed both palms to her cheeks. Her skin was warm. Maybe she was blushing. Was she already embarrassing herself, and he wasn't even here yet?

She tried again.

"I am Lyssena. You probably know that—"

No. No, no, no. Who says that?

She sounded ridiculous, like a girl trying to fill the silence with something—anything—but grace.

"Hello," she whispered, watching her mouth form the word in the mirror. "I am . . . grateful for your time?"

Gods. What if she just smiled and said nothing?

What if her lips twitched strangely and she looked like she was in pain? What if she laughed too loudly at something that wasn't even a joke? What if he had no sense of humor at all? What if—?

She groaned and flopped onto her bed, burying her face in her favorite pillow.

This was impossible.

She was the daughter of a good family, and yet a single sentence felt like a battlefield. Still, she rose again and smoothed her gown. She turned back to the mirror.

Because she had to get it right. Or at least, not get it wrong.

"Welcome to our home. I am honored to finally meet you."

Oh. That was better, she thought. That would sound very noble of her.

"My name is Lyssena, and—"

A knock at the door made Lyssena gasp. She turned toward it, hands flying to her chest.

Koren opened it slowly, his grin barely contained. He loved teasing his younger sister, and seeing her reaction was indeed very funny.

"Come, Lyss. Everything's ready, and your knight in shining armor is at the village gates."

She swallowed hard and rose to her feet, smoothing the front of her gown with trembling hands. Koren offered his arm with a small, dramatic bow, clearly trying to make her smile. She took it, yet her fingers were not quite as steady as his.

They walked together down the narrow hall, the wooden floors creaking beneath them. The air was warm with the scent of roasted meat and honey-glazed bread. As they turned the corner, the dining room came into view, and Lyssena's breath caught. She knew tonight was a great celebration, but she definitely did not expect her parents to spend so much coin they didn't have.

The long table had never been so finely dressed. Fresh bread steamed on carved platters. Bowls of berries and thick cream glistened beside roasted rabbits and spiced deer meat. A wreath of herbs hung from the beam overhead.

"There's our girl," Father said, his voice filled with pride.

Mother turned, already reaching out to adjust Lyssena's shoulders, though they needed no smoothing. "You look lovely."

Lyssena nodded. Words would not come. Her chest felt too tight.

Koren gave her arm a gentle squeeze before letting go, walking toward the table to join the others.

She inhaled slowly, trying to calm her heartbeat.

Then she heard hooves.

At first, just as a whisper, like wind stirring dry leaves. But the sound grew louder, deeper, and more solid. Her heart pounded so fiercely she was sure someone would hear it.

Outside, the sun had nearly vanished. The sky was painted in tones of burnt peach and bruised lilac, the last breath before night took hold. Shadows stretched long across the walls.

Lyssena edged toward the window, just close enough to peek past the curtain.

She saw the tail of a great, dark horse swishing in the dusky air. Just a flicker of movement. Just the edge of a presence. But it was real.

Kaan had arrived.

"Keep your head down, sweet one," her mother whispered as Lyssena rushed back to stand beside her. A hand settled gently on her back. "Let him come to you."

Then the front door creaked open.

There was no knock. Just the slow, groaning protest of the hinges, like someone entering a place they believed already belonged to them.

Lyssena froze.

Her pulse stumbled, her hands curled into the fabric of her gown. Her breath caught, and she refused to move.

He didn't knock. Why didn't he knock?

Her mother's hand remained on her spine, but Lyssena's

mind had already begun to spiral. The sound of boots met her ears. Not her father's. Not her brothers'. Heavier and very unfamiliar.

Her eyes stayed lowered.

Her heart thudded high in her chest.

And now everything began.

Chapter Three

A Lie of a Bargain

Lyssena

The door closed behind him.

Silence stretched between every step he took.

"You can look at your new owner."

Lyssena's eyes remained fixed on her feet, on the hem of the white gown she had felt so proud to wear only hours before. Now it trembled in time with her fingers.

"I'm waiting, Lyssena."

She blinked—once, twice—her mouth parting in disbelief. Surely he hadn't meant it like that. Surely it was a mistake, a cruel joke, or some tradition she hadn't yet learned.

But she didn't move. She simply couldn't.

"Go on," the knight said, this time louder. His tone was clipped and bored. The kind of voice used for servants, not for brides. "Raise your head. Let me see what I paid for."

Her stomach dropped like a stone tossed into still water. The taste of bile rose at the back of her throat. Sweat traced a path down the center of her spine, and another bead rolled along the curve of her temple, tickling her cheek like a tear that had come uninvited.

He paid.

The words echoed in her mind, again and again.

He paid.

A hand pressed gently to her back; it was her father's. The same hand that had steadied her when she was small, still afraid of the dark or the deep parts of the river.

"Come now, Lyss," he said softly. "Stand up straight. It's a proud night."

His voice was kind. But he had lied.

Lyssena thought both families exchanged a coin and some gifts. She knew that this was how marriage worked. She had hoped to bear many children to a man who would love her, and to come visit her family every few days. Lyssena prayed to all four gods for a good man and believed her family would do the same.

She believed her family would never lie.

Tears gathered at the base of her eyes as she lifted her head.

The man before her wore armor that might once have gleamed, but it was dulled with wear and dried blood. The metal was scuffed, smeared, likely signs of battle or . . . other things. Worse things.

His eyes were the kind of pale that looked blind, but they weren't. They were evil, unblinking, and hungry.

When he smirked, a scar stretched across his cheek like a wound pulling itself open.

"I expected more freckles," he said, gripping the hilt of his sword. "But I like the pale look. More delicate. Easier to bruise."

Behind her, one of her brothers let out a small, awkward laugh.

Something inside her pulled taut, too tight to breathe.

"Kaan," her father said, stepping slightly forward, his voice tight. "Perhaps . . . a gentler tone. She's still—"

"She's mine now, isn't she?" the man interrupted, never taking his eyes off her. "I paid well enough. Didn't I?"

Her father cleared his throat and rubbed his knuckles. "Well, yes, but—"

"Then I'll speak to her how I like. Break her in proper." Kaan waved a dismissive hand without turning. "You got your coin. Now keep your pride out of it."

Lyssena's vision blurred at the edges. The sweat on her skin turned cold.

He was supposed to smile.

He was supposed to take her hand. To say her name with a kind voice, the way her family always had. Instead, he stepped closer, and Lyssena flinched.

At that, his grin stretched wider. "Scared already?"

She couldn't breathe. Her eyes darted to her father, but he did not meet them. Her mother stared at the floor. All five of her brothers looked away.

Everyone had lied.

They had loved her, fed her, been kind to her, even as they prepared to sell her.

Those kind hands that once ruffled her hair were the same hands that handed the money and sold her like cattle.

She stepped back. Once. Then again. "You sold me," she whispered, her voice barely a breath.

Kaan laughed. "Come now," he said. "What good is a daughter if she can't be turned into a bargain?"

And just like that, Lyssena understood that the gods had never listened.

The four great gods she had knelt before since childhood—Kalos, Leyeer, Jenar, Syvaar—they had turned their backs on her. Not when she shouted. Not when she sinned. But when she was quiet. When she was kind. When she begged.

When she *never lied.*

Who did she belong to now?

Not her parents or brothers. Just her.

She took another step back until her spine met the wall behind her. The knight's grin widened further, that cruel gleam in his eyes rooting her to the spot.

She shifted, slipped sideways, and turned, moving down the hall that led to her room.

There was no one left to help her. No gods left to pray to.

She was alone.

"Lyssena!" the knight's voice barked behind her, but she didn't stop. She didn't turn.

There was one more god she could pray to.

Somewhere, deep inside her mind, she thought of the fifth candle. The one she had never dared to light. How do you pray to a god you do not know?

Please, she thought. You are my only chance. I beg you—

Tears slipped down her cheeks, falling freely as her trembling fingers closed around the door handle.

Why did they do this to her? Had she done anything wrong?

She always listened and always obeyed. She never lied . . .

But they did.

"Lyssena, come back here," snarled the voice of that horrid-looking knight, his words snapping through the hallway like a whip that promised to find her skin the moment she belonged to him. But she didn't belong to him; she couldn't, she wouldn't, and no voice, no threat, no man's coin could ever make that right in her soul.

She rounded the door and slammed it shut, the sound

cracking like thunder through her bones, and with every breath she threw herself against the bed, her entire weight driving it inch by inch across the wooden floor, though it was heavy and she was so tired and her stomach was empty, and her body shook with grief and fury and terror, and still the tears would not stop falling.

Who are you, fifth god? Let me pray to you. Please, let me pray.

A thunderous knock shook the door in its frame, and the bed creaked in protest beneath her straining limbs as she braced against it with her knees, her lower back aching, her breath a frantic rush between sobs.

"Go away!" she screamed, and she didn't recognize the sound of her own voice, raw and animal, something she had never heard from herself before, never in all her life.

Please help me, great fifth god, she pleaded in silence. *I don't know your name, I don't know how to speak to you, I don't even know if you listen, but if you do, if you've ever listened to anyone, listen to me now.*

"I will break that door if you don't open it!"

His voice crashed through the air like thunder, closer, louder, vicious and unrelenting, and Lyssena's eyes darted wildly around the room in search of anything to block the door, anything heavy to save her, to protect her. Her gaze snagged on the prayer desk, on the candles and the books she had cherished, and she knew she couldn't move it in time.

So she turned to the bookshelf, hands trembling uncontrollably as she grabbed every thick volume she could reach and tossed them onto the bed, stacking them high, as if the weight of stories and parchment and prayer could somehow shield her from the fury breaking toward her.

Please, fifth god, she begged. *If you are real, hear me now. I am begging. I am pleading. I am sorry I never lit your flame. I am sorry I never asked your name. But I ask now. Please. Please help me.*

A scream ripped from her throat as the door splintered, wood cracking like bones, and the knight crashed into the room with a monstrous force that knocked the air from her lungs as she fell hard on her back and hands, pain blooming sharp in her wrists as she scrambled to crawl backward across the floor.

Please let me know your name.

He strode toward her slowly, his face twisted in rage, his eyes burning wild and unhinged, and there was such hatred in his expression that it made her feel like she might come undone entirely, as if she could vanish into her own fear.

Her head struck the edge of the prayer desk, and she winced, blinking back the sharp pain, but her gaze locked instantly on the candle she had never lit—the fifth flame.

I have to light it. I have to do it now.

"You little bitch," the knight snarled, his voice thick with venom and gravel, "HOW DARE YOU!"

Her fingers fumbled across the surface of the desk, slick with sweat and trembling so violently she could hardly grip the flint, but she struck it once—nothing—again—sparks—and on the third strike, finally, a flame.

It caught slowly, reluctantly, the wick resisting the fire as if unsure it wanted to burn at all, but then it did.

And the fire was not gold.

It was dark like ink and blood and shadow, a flame that swallowed light instead of offering it.

The knight let out a cruel, barked laugh. "The gods won't help you," he spat, stepping closer with the certainty of a man who believed the world owed him its obedience. "They never do."

Lyssena pressed her palms together, breath ragged, limbs trembling, but she closed her eyes and whispered anyway.

Please . . . I don't know your name, but I offer myself, I offer my voice, I offer my soul if you want it—just save me. Save me from him.

She pleaded so hard she couldn't hear the man standing before her. She pleaded so hard she couldn't even notice how the knight was already standing right in front of her face.

Erevos.

Her eyes snapped open. "What?" she whispered aloud, blinking as if the name had struck her from within.

The knight paused, his hand hanging above his chest, his brows furrowing. "What did you say?"

"I . . . I didn't . . ."

They stared at each other, both of them confused.

My name is Erevos.

Chapter Four

Born From a Broken Prayer

Erevos

She had begged for a god, so he became one.

When the little human whispered into the dark, her voice thin with grief and breaking at the edges, he felt the moment her faith splintered, and because he had always been drawn to broken things, he listened.

The others had turned their faces away, content with their temples and songs and the prayers of the living, satisfied with incense and sacrifice and the rhythm of breath unbroken. But he, Erevos, heard what they refused to; he fed on what they would not touch.

He had felt her despair before she ever lit the flame, and when she did, he tasted it. It was divine, raw, and oh-so-delicious.

The instant her soul cracked, the moment her knees struck the floor and her breath hitched in her throat like something caught between sob and scream, he knew she had called him. Not by name, not aloud, but in the oldest language: devotion.

And so he came.

The male's hand stretched toward her, fingers filthy and greedy, curled as if to drag her by the hair. But Erevos had already arrived.

He sent his shadows along the splintered wood and the cracked stone, a dark tide slithering across the walls until it reached the man whose mouth still moved—still speaking, still vulgar—until his jaw jerked open with a strangled gasp as tendrils of smoke coiled around his throat like something alive. He tried to scream, or maybe even tried to pray.

But it was too late.

He was not hers. He did not matter.

Behind the man, Erevos rose, shadows building and writhing, slithering into grotesque formations and half-shapes, flickering between forms no living mind was meant to witness, let alone name—and then, he devoured.

His mass spilled outward, over the floor, into the beams, like ink coursing through veins too thin to hold, and when he constricted, the man's spine cracked with a sound that almost became a song. Erevos loved the sound of dying prey: when the body flailed, flesh split, and bone shattered.

And Lyssena watched.

Her eyes were wide, wet, and wild with terror. Though he had no eyes now, only presence, only weight and shadow and a strong hunger that might have just devoured her too, he felt her gaze, felt her silence curl around the edges of what he was.

She tasted of belief and agony, of milk and honey.

Lyssena scrambled back, even where there was nowhere to crawl. Crawling in place, trembling, her gown wrinkled and her cheeks streaked with tears.

"I heard you," he said, voice low and everywhere at once. "And I came."

While the small, shivering woman before him wrestled

with the impossible, still deciding whether he was real or not, he gathered the pieces of the broken door. His shadows slid across the floor, dragging splinters on uneven wood. The door groaned as it returned to place, fitted by unseen hands and sealed.

He sensed her family before they spoke. Their stuttered heartbeats, the sharp breaths, the tang of fear flooding their bloodstreams. He could map their limbs by the rhythm of it.

"Lyssena? Lyssena!"

The voice was her father's. Foolish, not brave, calling her name as if she still belonged to him.

Erevos might not have understood why her family would show that they cared after what they had done. But he knew it didn't matter.

What mattered to him was the small human named Lyssena, staring at him with wide eyes and trembling fingers.

"What's going on in there? Open the door!"

Fists struck his shadows, which had hardened to stone.

"Lyssena, answer me!"

"Please, gods—Lyss, please!"

"Open this door!"

The noise was loud, their pleading sincere. But they could not reach her anymore. Erevos has already decided that she was his. She, however, had not yet decided what to think of him, and Erevos did not rush her to answer.

He had all the time in the world, as he had been living for so long already. A creature so ancient as he was would not care for screams and fear of mortals he did not care about. He never cared for anyone, really, but this human named Lyssena had caught his hungry soul.

"Who . . . who are you?" she asked, her voice hoarse, small, barely more than a breath shaped into sound.

"I am Erevos," he answered, as shadows spilled from him

like ink, coating every surface of the room—the floor, the walls, the bed, and desk—until all that remained was void. "I am the one you called."

Erevos did not know why she would ask such a question, as he had already told her his name and had come when she called. But he was patient with her. He gave her time to think and reflect.

Lyssena turned her gaze to the blackened room, eyes wide, whispering, "You're not . . . like the others."

"No," he said. Those absent gods, those hollow idols humans created for themselves to hang onto something when they needed. "I am not made of harvests or light, nor of coin or prayer. I am the dark beneath the altar. I am the echo that never fades."

"I didn't mean to . . . I didn't know if you were real."

"And yet, you lit the flame," he said, shadows flickering as he drew closer. "You begged for someone to listen. I did. You gave your devotion shape. You called, and I answered."

She said nothing after that. Lyssena only sat there, draped in a white gown, one arm bracing her weight, the other resting on her thigh. Her hair—light brown and unbound—cascaded in soft waves down her back and across her shoulders, reaching her thighs like a veil spun from dusk. With those green eyes, wide and full of sorrow and fear, she looked like a herta, the kind once kept in homes back in his homeland. He knew it looked like the cats humans had in this world.

Lyssena's mind screamed.

He could feel the spiral of it, tearing at itself from within. Guilt, grief, and confusion rose beneath her silence.

Beyond the walls of shadow, her family still cried out. Voices loud, feet thudding against wood. One of her brothers shouted her name again and again. And when she flinched,

Erevos added more shadows of his to the walls and the shadow-maid door.

She turned toward the sound. "My family . . ."

"They sold you, Lyssena," he said. "They set a price on your blood and handed you to the slaughterhouse with smiles on their lips. They called it love so you would kneel more willingly."

"But they . . . they fed me, they cared for me . . ."

"You think a cage is not a cage because the bars were kissed before they closed?"

She turned her face away, and tears slipped silently down her cheeks.

Erevos was not sure why she suddenly started defending those who wronged her. But he didn't always understand human ways. And so he decided to finally tell her.

"You have a choice," he said. "To stay, or to leave."

Her eyes widened. Slowly, she turned her gaze toward the shadowed wall where once there had been a window.

"How can I leave them?" she whispered, her heart thundering so loudly that he wished to come closer and feel it himself.

"The family that betrayed you?" he asked. "The ones who watched you tremble and said nothing while he reached for your throat?"

She shook her head, slowly, as if the motion pained her. "I don't know what to believe anymore."

"Then believe *me*," Erevos said. "Come with me, Lyssena. Leave this house of hollow love and poisoned mercy."

He had watched her for a long time.

He had memorized the way her fingers lingered on the rim of a cup, the movement of her throat when she swallowed. He had counted each bite she took, noted which foods made her eyes close in pleasure, which textures made her flinch. He had learned what she needed to survive—bread, water, warmth—and he had committed to memory the names of every object her hands had ever cherished. He had done so to rebuild them, to offer them back.

Human devotion was never the same from one soul to the next.

But *hers*, hers was woven with longing and light, fragile and searing. It was the most exquisite devotion he had ever hungered for.

She hesitated, and he waited, because he had all the time in the world.

"Come with me, Lyssena, and I shall become your god."

Chapter Five

The Meaning of Devotion

Lyssena

She sat on nothing.

There was no floor beneath her, only the suggestion of one. A flat impression drawn in shadow, as if the world had been dipped in ink and left to dry wrong. Her palm rested against that void, sinking slightly, but there was no texture, no grain, only the eerie sensation of pressing against a thought, something that wasn't truly there and yet insisted on being felt.

Everything was wrong.

The walls, the bed, the very air had been dipped in shadow. Shapes remained: the outline of the dresser, the sharp angle of the door frame, the familiar rise of her bed, but they were now hollow sketches and painted in pitch. And at the center of it all: him.

A living mass of black, shifting and pulsing, the suggestion of form where no form should exist. He had no true edges, only movement like smoke that understood how to hold itself together.

Then, his eyes opened.

Two perfect purple orbs that stretched backward, and her mind, despite everything, longed toward prayer. But she did not move.

Because something was changing again.

The darkness that was Erevos began to draw inward, folding and condensing, and time seemed to slow to match the rhythm of his becoming. His height—too vast to belong within the narrow confines of her room—compressed until it could fit. Shoulders took shape, broad and thick, as if chiseled from the dark before light had ever been born. His chest followed, muscles like slabs of stone wrapped in something that pretended to be skin. Lyssena wasn't sure whether to be scared or fascinated.

Erevos was massive.

Every muscle looked like it had been forged before softness had entered the world, each tendon flexing with restrained violence. His thighs stretched wide, thick and solid and entirely without mercy, carved from the kind of strength men could only dream of. This was not a man. This was the thing men imagined when they wished to be feared.

And last came his face. The head of a man, but featureless. No mouth, no nose, only those eyes, those endless, watching purple eyes.

Her family's voices, still clawing from the other side of the shadow-walls, began to fade, swallowed slowly as the room darkened further—if such a thing were even possible.

He watched her, and she watched him.

He waited, and Lyssena could not comprehend what was happening before her. She has already forgotten the horrid knight named Kaan. She didn't notice the screams outside the new door. She only thought of what had just happened.

She had prayed. She had called for a god, and now he had come, asking her to go with him. But what did that mean? What did it mean to go with a god like this?

Was she going to die?

"I don't want to die," she whispered, and she finally realized she was speaking to a real god.

She should kneel. Her body knew that, even if her heart did not. Had she forgotten how to show respect so quickly?

She moved slowly, folding her legs beneath her, pressing her weight onto her arms as she righted herself into a posture of obedience. She placed her palms gently on her thighs and lowered her gaze.

Besides being a god, he was a male, and she could not meet his eyes now, not now that she had seen that he had them. He was a god, and she must show respect.

Lyssena was afraid, and yet she was not.

She did not know what to do.

"Why would you die?" Erevos asked, and she felt the shift of his presence as he moved away from her, soundless but felt, a displacement in the air that made her want to look up, to follow him with her eyes, to know what he was doing, but she didn't.

She mustn't.

"You said you want to take me with you . . . " she murmured, voice trembling.

"Does that mean you would die?"

How could she have asked that? How dare she question him? Foolish, foolish Lyssena. She had never spoken to a god before—at least she had never heard back—had never even dreamed of being in the presence of one. He could do as he pleased with her.

So she kept her eyes down, head bowed, because it felt right, because her body had unraveled into the shape of a prayer, and for once—just once—it wasn't for someone who had never listened.

They hadn't listened.

Not when she was a child, sick with fear, praying with tiny hands clenched over her heart that her mother's cough would go away. Not when she asked for the goats to stop dying so they might have milk to sell. Not when she whispered into her pillow, night after night, asking for safety, or love, or a gentle husband. *They* were silent.

They had always been silent.

They gave nothing.

But *he* came.

And that truth was clear to her.

She could not understand it the way she would want to. But he had heard her. She had lit the flame and screamed inside, and he had torn through the veil between worlds to stand between her and the man who would have broken her. And he had not waited for gratitude, had not asked for ritual, before erasing the threat.

That was strength. That was a god.

She exhaled slowly and lowered herself further, pressing her forehead to the ground—though there was no true ground here, only shadow—but it felt like him, as if every surface now bore his name. The air, the floor, the weight in her chest —it was all Erevos. She folded forward, smaller and smaller, arms at her sides, palms open, spine bowed so low she felt the pull at the base of her skull, and still she did not raise her head.

She had never felt this small and never this safe.

Erevos. Erevos. Erevos.

There was no holy room. No elder's voice telling her what

she owed and how to say it. There were no temple rules, no rituals she needed to memorize. There was only this: her truth.

This god came when the others didn't.

And for that alone, he deserved everything she had been taught to give and more. If devotion had weight, she would give all of hers to him. If faith had shape, she would mold it in his image.

Around her, the shadows pulsed. It was soft, like breath taken slowly. It felt warmer, with something deeper that wrapped itself around her gently, curling into the hollows behind her knees, the arch of her spine, like night falling softly over a weary world.

How could she ever express her gratitude?

So she offered more.

She whispered, "You're the only one who ever came. Please, greatest Erevos . . . take me with you."

And it was the holiest thing she had ever said.

Lyssena opened her eyes and felt well-rested. Though she could not remember the moment she had fallen asleep, and as she glanced down, she discovered herself wrapped in a thick black blanket, lying on a bed just as dark. Everything about it was unfamiliar and yet . . . gentle.

Is this my room?

Lyssena turned her head slowly, letting her gaze sweep across the space, and saw that everything around her existed in shades of black. One flat color, but within it layers, depths, textures that felt as though the dark had moods and temperatures and names she had never learned.

It felt like a cave, but nothing like the ones from the forest near her house. The walls here were strange, curling into fluid shapes that had no corners. There was no light except for something above her that glowed faintly.

She tilted her head back and found a single orb suspended high above, casting a dim, gray light that barely dared to exist. It was the first hint of color she had seen since waking, and even that seemed shy.

She sat up slowly, fingers running across the surface of the blanket. It was soft, thicker than linen, gentler than wool, not fur, not anything she could easily name, and the strangeness of its texture made her hum without meaning to, just a quiet sound of thought as her eyes moved toward the far side of the room.

Another wall. Black again.

She lifted her hand, reached toward it, and pressed her fingers against the surface, feeling something cold and solid. The question echoed again in her mind: *Where am I?*

"Do you breathe well?" a voice asked, echoing through the walls. "Tell me where it feels wrong. I will adjust it."

Erevos.

She froze, hand still against the wall, and lowered her head instinctively. Lyssena wasn't sure what he meant by adjusting. The air? Well, he was a god. Perhaps he could really do anything. And still she was confused.

"I breathe well. Thank you," she said, her voice quiet, her thumb rubbing against the other.

"You may walk," Erevos said. "Touch what you wish. See if this place suits you."

She hesitated, then rose.

Her steps were almost silent. She was hesitant about everything around her. Lyssena's fingertips brushed against the back of a high-backed chair, which was shaped exactly like the one that had stood by her window at home. It even had the same faint curve at the top, the one she used to drape her shawl across in the early evening.

She blinked, frowning, her gaze drifting toward the dresser beside it.

She knew that shape.

The edge was slightly worn on the left side, just as it had been at home, where she had once spilled oil and tried to scrub it clean, only to fade the color instead. Her fingers moved to the second drawer, and sure enough, the handle pulled out a little too far, the screw loose in the same, familiar way.

The way the bed was placed, tucked beneath a low curve in the ceiling, looked like her room.

Not exactly, but close enough that her heart began to beat faster. She turned in place. There had been a pillow she loved, one she always held when she couldn't stop her thoughts from circling, but it wasn't here.

And then it was.

It appeared so quickly, without sound or movement, nestled in the corner of the bed, as dark as everything else in this place, but unmistakably shaped like the one she used to cling to beneath the covers when the night stretched too long, and the world felt too sad.

She gasped and stepped back.

I didn't say that out loud.

The pillow looked wrong at first—slightly off, not square—and she moved closer. She reached out, fingers trembling as they brushed its surface. And then she saw five edges. Not four.

She had torn it as a child, by accident, playing too roughly, too carelessly, and tried to sew it back together herself. She had been too small, her stitches uneven, and the whole corner had collapsed in her hands. So she had added a new one. A fifth edge. It wasn't perfect, but it had made the pillow feel whole again. No one else had known. No one else had ever noticed.

And now it sat before her.

Then came the vibrating sound that filled the room, like an animal's growl, and she clapped her hands over her ears out of fear, heart slamming into her ribs. But it didn't help; she could still hear it, not through her ears, but somewhere deeper.

Inside her head.

Chapter Six

Little Songbird

Erevos

This little mortal amused Erevos, and he was pleased.

He had thought her bones too soft, her mind too delicate, her prayers too beautiful when they reached the deep where he dwelled. And yet she had reached him. She had called, and when she did, she offered something most mortals no longer knew how to give—devotion. So raw, it was so beautiful to him. And now, she stood within the space he had created, gasping when the walls remembered her shape, when the air curved itself to feel like home.

That pleased him.

He had studied her world long before he ever touched it.

He had slipped through the floorboards and the folds of her dreams. He had memorized the slight wear on the stool she perched on when she thought no one was watching, the faint oil stain on her dresser left by accident, the imperfect seam in the curtain she had sewn herself, the shallow dent in the bed frame from the press of her heel while she read. He knew how her fingers lingered on wood, how she smoothed the edges of fabric when her thoughts wandered, how her breath changed just before she turned a page.

So he had recreated them.

Not as illusions, but as offerings for this little human.

He wove her room from shadow and memory, and sculpted it detail by detail until the darkness bent itself to resemble what she had once known. When she woke, he had not wanted her to be lost. Her world had betrayed her; he would not. He would become what was familiar, and then, in time, he would become more.

But structure alone would never be enough.

She must be *kept*.

He could still feel the hum of fear in her head, though she tried to mask it with a lowered gaze. Her skin—he could sense it —longed for warmth and comfort.

A bath, he thought, the idea blooming in his mind. Her body would respond to heat, to steam curling across skin. Yes, he would give her that. A bath, first. A beginning.

And then food.

Something that would not startle her, something warm that tasted of honey and safety. Something that invited trust.

She had loved books.

He remembered how she turned pages in silence, her lips moving as she read, her whole world narrowed to the shape of language. Words had power in her life, like companions. She carried them gently, like friends she could rely on. He would bring her books even if he had to tear them from the false temples of gods who were never real.

She must feel welcomed. No, not welcomed. She must feel *chosen.*

Because she had been, and though her voice had trembled, and her eyes had filled with tears, she had chosen him back.

Erevos looked upon his little human and thought she resembled a songbird from the world of humans, like the ones he had seen inside cages they carried: feathered things with bright eyes and trembling hearts, trapped within bars. It reminded him of her. Of little Lyssena, who had always been a pretty songbird in a pretty cage. Cared for, but never free; fed, but never truly full; loved, but never unconditionally. If her name hadn't been Lyssena, he thought he might have named her songbird, and that notion, absurd and tender all at once, filled him with something warm and soft, something close to joy.

When his little songbird finally settled into the chair, Erevos decided she had finished exploring the space he had made for her, and so he began to wonder how to ask what came next. But he hesitated.

Should he ask whether she would prefer a bath first, then food after? Or perhaps she would want nourishment now, and something else later?

In his studies of her routines, he had observed that she bathed at varied times. Sometimes upon waking, sometimes just before slipping into sleep, and occasionally after returning from her tasks, when her arms ached from carrying baskets full of goods. There was no fixed pattern he could rely on, and it left him uncertain.

Humans, after all, were so very bound by rules.

Rules about when to eat, when to sleep, when to speak, when to mourn, when to smile. So many, layered atop one another, and he had never cared enough to count them.

"Would you like to bathe?" he finally asked.

She looked up, just a little, and then shook her head. Not a refusal born of fear, he thought, as he didn't feel any, but perhaps the simple need for something else.

"Then tell me," he said gently, "what do you want?"

"I would want some food, please."

There it was, so simple and honest. Creatures like himself did not often comprehend the constant mortal need for nourishment. He was not flesh, he did not wither or tire. Erevos was a demon born of shadow. He fed on devotion and the fractured souls of those who had been left behind.

And yet, after following his little songbird through her days, he had begun to understand just how different they were. Where he consumed belief like fire consumes air, she needed warmth, sustenance, and repetition. She needed meals not for hunger alone, but also for the comfort they carried. For the way steam rises from a fine bowl or the scent of honey on fresh bread. He had seen humans enjoy the bread without honey, too, so adding this new flavor was at first confusing. And now, after so many years of watching, he knew.

Erevos did not move yet, though he would go soon. He would shape her a meal with his own shadows, that would not frighten her—a comfort offering, perhaps spiced with honey or cinnamon. But before he left, he wished to give her something to hold her until he returned.

From his palm, he drew forth a piece of shadow, pliable and smooth, dark as ink before it touches parchment. He held it out to her, and the shape hovered above his hand, not quite alive, but not inert either.

"For you," he said. "It will bend to your fingers. Twist it, shape it, fold it until it becomes something that matters to you. It will not break unless you ask it to."

She reached out hesitantly, and as her fingers curled around it, the shadow moved in answer. Erevos nearly groaned from the pleasure of her touching him, but he didn't. He didn't want to frighten her.

"A distraction," he added. "Because silence, when left alone, becomes too loud."

And he watched her cradle the gift, watched her stare at it as it shifted in her palms, already beginning to become something else—what, he did not know.

But it was hers now, and it was a part of him.

And that, too, pleased him dearly.

Chapter Seven

Princess of Shadow

Lyssena

There was a dark room that did not move, and dark furniture that stayed still. But there was also something dark that shifted and responded, something that took shape each time Lyssena changed it. She wasn't sure whether it was some kind of divine clay gifted by her god, or perhaps a living creature pretending to be still. And because she could not tell for certain, she didn't tear it apart to see what was inside. Instead, she changed the shape as a whole and watched how it moved.

Lyssena shaped it into a chicken, and the small ball of shadow—of god-clay, perhaps, began to strut and cluck like one, head bobbing just like a real chicken. She molded it into a snake, and it curled around her wrist and hissed, tongue flicking out as if it knew how to threaten.

It was a sight to behold.

And in the quiet corner of her thoughts, she allowed herself a secret. She felt, just a little, like a small god. She was mending forms and giving breath to shadows, shaping something that should not be alive and yet was. She did not know how it worked, but whatever it was, it held her fascination entirely.

As the god's clay became a chicken, a snake, a pig, and even a piece of fruit beneath her curiosity, Lyssena had an idea. She gathered the shadows into a ball and began to mold them, flattening the shape, weaving a hole through the center, then lifting the edges gently to rise. When she finished, the god's clay had taken the shape of a crown.

"Would you listen if I asked you to have a shining light?" she whispered to the obsidian crown resting in her palms. And to her surprise, at the tips of the dark, curved points, small stones appeared—glinting softly, faint stars set in shadow. Lyssena didn't think they were real diamonds or rubies, but the sight of them stole her breath, and she gasped in awe before lifting the crown and placing it upon her head.

When Lyssena was a child, she had once wanted to be a princess. She would wrap herself in layers of curtains, fashion a cape from her mother's old shawl, walk proudly around her room with a stick she found outside as her scepter, and a makeshift crown of folded paper perched upon her brow. Once, her eldest brother Koren even pretended to be a horse, and she sat atop his back, laughter in her chest, feeling for that one bright afternoon like a fierce and powerful princess of her own little realm.

And that memory made her eyes wet.

They betrayed me.

The thought pained her so much, she shut her eyes so no tears would spill down her face.

She stood, moving slowly with the crown on her head, and walked to the edge of the room where the shadows thickened.

One hand brushed the curved wall. It was cool, smooth, but yielded slightly under her touch.

Lyssena had believed that family meant love. She believed she was safe if she never lied—and she never did.

She saw what consequences looked like when people lied. She had seen several women in her life being dragged behind the temple. It was a horrible sight, one that she would never, ever dare to forget.

One of them was a friend of Lyssena. A girl named Nora. At that time, they were fifteen.

Nora never lied, as most people did, but there was just this one time when she simply had to. Lyssena noticed the way Nora would sneak outside her home at night, thinking no one would see her. She suspected that Nora had perhaps met with a suitor. Why else would a woman her age sneak past her parents' eyes and judgment?

The third time, Lyssena saw the execution of Nora the next morning. She cried for days and nights, thinking of the possibilities of what she could have done to prevent that.

That gloomy morning, the priest said that Nora had sinned. That Nora lied to her parents.

That Nora will never lie again.

Lyssena trailed her fingers along the wall as she circled the room, her bare feet dragging over the darkened floor.

"They had not stopped him. They had not stood between the man who reached for my throat and me. They sold me, smiled, said I would be happy . . . and then didn't even look me in the eyes."

Stomping her feet, Lyssena let out a low, broken groan. She couldn't believe how her life had turned, twisted in on itself, all within the span of a few hours.

Her head snapped toward a sound, a knock. In this room, there were no doors, no windows; nothing to knock on.

At first, she thought she'd imagined it.

She took a slow step back, steadying the crown on her head with one hand, her fingers pressing gently against its side. Then it came again.

Another knock.

Her heart began to pound harder. Dread curled up her spine like a slow, reaching vine. *If it were Erevos, she thought, he wouldn't knock. He would appear just like he did before.*

She still wasn't sure where she was—this place of darkness —and she had planned to ask him when he returned. But she had not expected a knock.

She realized then just how distracted she'd been by the god's clay, by her grief, by the sting of betrayal. She hadn't even thought to consider the larger questions. She had forgotten, entirely, that she might no longer be in her village. That this space didn't belong to the world she once knew.

She hadn't wondered if gods lived in villages, as humans did, or in temples, or perhaps in the sky.

What if I'm truly in the sky?

The thought tightened something in her gut. She trusted Erevos; she had offered herself freely, but now, standing in a silent room with no doors or windows, no sky above her, and a knock coming from nowhere, Lyssena felt a flicker of doubt rise from beneath her certainty.

Not fear of *him.* But fear of how far from home she had come.

"Are you a human?"

The voice was muffled, echoing from somewhere beyond the shadow-woven walls, and Lyssena tried to remain calm— but she couldn't. Her chest tightened with fear, her breath shallowed, and dread rose beneath her skin. She was terrified that whoever—or whatever—was speaking would tear through the still walls of her god's sanctuary while Erevos was away, off doing whatever divine, unknowable things gods did when they vanished.

Was that another god? Or perhaps something else, something other. She was almost certain it wasn't human; the voice lacked the warmth, the weight, the shape that human voices carried. It felt wrong, not harsh or cruel, but hollow.

She needed to think—and fast.

Her crown slipped slightly, tilting forward against her brow, and in the moment of movement, she gasped, startled, and muffled it quickly with her own palm as she slapped it over her mouth.

She thought, for half a breath, to will the crown into a weapon, but quickly realized it wouldn't work. It was too small, and the god's clay she was given, for all its wonder, had limits. It would not, *could* not, become something so large.

So she turned her gaze outward.

Around her, the bed, far too heavy to lift; the dresser, even heavier. But the chair . . . the chair seemed manageable, light enough to move, and just solid enough to serve.

With trembling hands, she adjusted her crown and walked toward the chair. She wrapped her fingers around its back and held her breath. If the crown could change, perhaps the chair could too.

She closed her eyes and prayed.

Lyssena prayed from the base of her throat, from the hollow of her ribs, from the place inside her that knew how to kneel and beg and believe. She prayed that the chair would become something more.

And again, to her astonishment, it did.

The shape began to shift under her grip, the wooden curves melting into a bat, dark and crude. It was too heavy for her, far heavier than she had expected, but she held on with all the strength her arms could muster. Her knuckles went white, her shoulders tensed, but still she lifted it upright and set it before her.

Her pulse pounded in her ears; she had no idea what was coming.

But at least she would not be empty-handed.

Chapter Eight

The Songbird in the Void

Erevos

Erevos noticed that he was unusually warm.

It was not a sensation he typically experienced. Demons, by nature, did not grow warm on their own. Warmth was for blood and breath and beating hearts, for creatures made of flesh, not for beings like him. In his world, the place mortals called *The Void*, warmth was an anomaly. Creatures who dwelled there were always cool.

The Void itself was a strange place, especially to human eyes, a near mimicry of Earth, but not quite. There were trees the color of wine, and their bark was darker than midnight. There were rivers and ponds, but they ran black as ink, and anyone looking to seek their reflection would find only more endless black. There was no sun in The Void, no stars to catch the edge of light, no breeze to stir the air, no oxygen to fill human lungs. Nothing lived in The Void as mortals understood life. It was a realm of darkness and silence so deep it could become sound.

To most humans, The Void would seem deathless and strange, but to Erevos, it was home.

And now, he intended to make it *hers* as well.

So he walked through the silence while his warmth cooled off, toward a place few ever dared to approach, for the demon that resided there was unpleasant in both form and temperament, known to twist truths into poisons and smile while doing it. It was said he was cruel without reason.

That did not concern Erevos.

He did not flinch from cruelty, nor beauty, nor the in-between. He had come with a purpose. And he intended to feed his little mortal songbird. To nourish her, to provide her with anything she would ever need.

Erevos approached the mouth of a cave, one far beyond the reaches of where only a few demons of his kind chose to roam. It lay at the outer edges of The Void, where the land curled in on itself, and the shadows grew thick enough to muffle sound: a place rarely visited, and seldom without reason.

In The Void, a demon would take residence in a cave only for a few reasons.

The first: the demon was sick and could no longer fend for itself.

The second: the demon had adopted an animal—rare, but not unheard of—and the creature was either unwell or birthing.

The third: trade.

Unlike the human world, The Void did not deal in coin or cloth or the glittering trifles mortals seemed to prize. There was no currency in silk, no market for gold. In The Void, demons bartered in emotions. Feelings harvested, shaped, and distilled into items that carried weight and taste and memory. Traders would travel to the human world to collect such offerings—tears, laughter, longing—drawn into vials, pearls, and strange, shimmering fragments of light or dark.

For demons, visiting the human realm was a task few enjoyed. Mortals were rarely of interest outside of their use as nourishment, and fewer still were the demons willing to linger among the noise and rituals of their kind. Why attend a funeral to collect grief when one could simply trade for a weeping eye, still warm with sorrow? Why chase a grieving widow through her crumbling home when the ache of her loss could be traded, neatly packaged at the market?

Demons preferred simplicity.

But Erevos was not heading to the market. He was going farther. Beyond the trading circles. Beyond the more palatable vendors.

He was headed to the cave of a different kind of trader.

Rolam.

A name spoken only in private, if at all. A demon who dealt in rarer goods, stranger things. And while most void-born had little interest in the human world beyond what could be consumed, Rolam was different. He collected. And though Erevos had never lingered long in Rolam's presence, he had once seen some of what the strange demon had gathered— spices from distant earth markets, preserved organs, strands of human hair, and other things Erevos had never bothered to understand or value until now.

Because now he had a little songbird to care for. A mortal. And Erevos had seen her eat, watched her choose food with warmth and sweetness, watched her avoid sorrow and fear as though she could taste them just like he could.

She would not eat tears of grief. She would not chew the bubbles of fear demons loved. She needed something else. And Rolam, he hoped, would have it.

"Greetings, Erevos," Rolam mused, lounging in a chair that looked like it had been taken from a human tavern.

All demons knew one another. There weren't many of

them to begin with. None remembered where they had come from, and none had seen new demons born. They simply existed—always had—and no more ever appeared.

Erevos nodded to the demon across from him. Rolam was a creature as dark as he was, though his eyes were larger, purple orbs that glimmered faintly in the half-light.

Beside Rolam, a herta stretched its long limbs, extending its fuzzy paws with a kind of lazy grace. It was a Void-creature, catlike but not quite, its fur rippling with shadow. As Erevos crossed the threshold of the cave, the herta rolled onto its side and exposed its belly.

"Got interested in humans, have you?" Rolam asked, his voice a rasping purr, his gaze following Erevos as he moved deeper into the cavernous store. The place was dark, as most corners of The Void were, lit only by orbs of suspended light. Each one pulsed softly with contained emotion. Some glowed red with rage, some blue with sorrow, some pulsed gold with longing. Erevos passed one strange orb and paused.

Within it shimmered a translucent-white liquid; the scent was rather sweet.

Erevos stilled, and that strange warmth returned, rising deep in his chest. He turned his gaze briefly toward the orb, then looked away.

"I want to feed a human," he said at last.

Rolam tilted his head, "A human?"

Erevos knew it sounded odd, even for a collector like Rolam, but he did not flinch or offer an explanation either.

No one knew he was keeping a human, and no one would believe it was even possible. Mortals did not survive in The Void. There was no oxygen for them to breathe, and even if there were, demons did not protect humans—they fed on their emotions. That was the order of things.

And yet.

He nodded once more to the puzzled trader, who studied him with hollow eyes. Rolam turned away without further comment and wandered through his collection, running long fingers over vials and jars and shadow-wrapped containers, until his gaze landed on a small, bone-colored box.

Erevos noticed traces of another presence near the cave he had chosen for his human, traces that were not his own, which made them all the more troubling. He had made certain to leave no evidence of his passage, not even a whisper of scent that might linger in the dark. There should have been no reason for another demon to follow him, no cause for any creature to inspect a cave that bore the scent of ownership. In The Void, there were many caves, each available to whoever had the power to keep them, so the fact that someone had come near this one made no sense at all.

And so, he rushed.

He descended deep into the winding corridors of shadow, navigating through countless entrances branching in different directions, until he finally arrived at the chamber he had shaped where his little songbird waited. The bone-colored box was cradled in his shadow as he stepped into the perimeter of his crafted haven, and without hesitation, he merged with the shadowed walls.

"Lyssena?" he called, echoing through the dim chamber.

He did not see her, but he felt her scent that was laced with fear. He followed the pull of her presence and paused when his gaze landed on the bed, but something was wrong.

Erevos detached from the walls, allowing his form to build itself piece by piece—legs forming first, long and stable, then his torso, arms, shoulders, and at last, his head. He placed the box upon the desk, though even that looked wrong now—different from the one he had crafted for her. He turned to the bed, which no longer looked quite like the bed he had shaped, and when he lifted it, he found her.

His little human was curled beneath it, trembling, her breath uneven. She had surrounded herself with items, shadows, and remnants twisted into weapons, and on her head sat a crown made of his shadow.

Erevos had not expected this.

Not the fear or the fortress, which was a surprise as well, but the armored queen beneath the bed.

Chapter Nine

To Look Upon a God

Lyssena

After Lyssena asked the bed to become a place to hide, it did. At some point, she stopped gasping in awe each time the shadows obeyed her. She began to accept it, to expect it, to use it for her own need.

The chair had become a weapon, a bat heavy enough to steady her grip but not too heavy to wield. The bed had folded itself into a hollow haven. The desk had shifted, grown broad and curved, becoming a shield between her and the unknown.

The room no longer looked like the one Erevos had created. "Songbird?"

Before she could register that it was Erevos speaking, she let out a scream. As the sound tore from her throat, her crown tumbled from her head, falling onto the dark floor. Her heart slammed against her ribs with such force she thought she might simply die right there beneath the bed that was not a bed anymore, surrounded by weapons of her own making.

But then the shadows deepened. The darkness around her

grew darker, denser, as if it recognized him before she did. Slowly, she lifted her head by instinct, and then she remembered she wasn't supposed to look directly at a god. Or at a male at that.

Her gaze dropped again, her body folding smaller in apology.

Erevos knelt before her, and she saw his knee—black as the void itself—press against the floor. Everything seemed darker, as though his presence made the shadows real again. When her crown had fallen, she'd heard it strike something hard, a sound that surprised her. The floor had softened in his absence, like everything else. But now that he was here, the room remembered what it was supposed to be.

A long minute passed in silence, and slowly, her heart settled back into rhythm. It no longer drowned out her thoughts.

Because her god had returned, and if Erevos was here, then surely, surely everything would be fine.

He picked up the crown from the floor, rubbed it gently between his fingers, and, without a word, placed it back on her head.

"Why were you so scared?" he asked.

His voice was very kind, and Lyssena, in that moment, wondered if this was a test—a test of faith, of truth. Because Erevos was a god, was he not? He must have already known the answer. Gods knew everything. They knew so much that humans would've never comprehended the vastness of their greatness.

Perhaps he was testing her honesty, or her loyalty. Either way, she saw no reason to lie.

She had never lied—not to anyone.

And she would *never* lie to her god.

She wanted to understand him, to learn her place in this

strange and shifting place that no longer looked like the room it had once been. She wanted to know what he expected of her, how she might serve him, how she might prove herself worthy of the power she had borrowed and the room she had been given.

"I was scared because someone was waiting outside," Lyssena answered. And it was the truth. She had been truly, deeply afraid. Afraid that the strange presence beyond the walls would tear through the soft, living shadows and seize her by the throat, would drag her out and devour her while her god was still away, too far to stop it.

She had been afraid that Erevos wouldn't return in time.

Afraid that she would die in a place she didn't understand.

Afraid that she had accomplished nothing with the life she was given by the parents who betrayed her.

Lyssena had always been a simple girl with simple dreams and a simple life. She had cooked, cleaned, and completed every chore that was handed to her without complaint. She had shown kindness to others and even met a few people she could call friends. Her world had been small, but it had been hers— until the moment it wasn't.

Until the moment her family turned their backs on her.

And they had done it at the exact moment she'd felt her happiest. When she thought her life might finally be unfolding into something bright.

Maybe Lyssena hadn't been so simple after all.

Because now she had a god.

"I hope I have not offended you with my staring . . ." She murmured, her voice quiet with shame, her gaze once more lowered to the floor. She hadn't meant to—truly hadn't—, but in her despair, she had forgotten herself. Forgotten the rules. Forgotten the fear of failing again.

She had failed to build the life she wanted, and now, perhaps, she was failing here too.

"What do you mean by offended?" Erevos asked, and Lyssena's breath caught.

She didn't know how to answer. She wasn't sure if he didn't understand the word, or if he was testing her again, pushing her to confess her faults.

And so—quietly, with trembling hands—she did.

"I dared to lift my gaze to your greatness," she whispered.

A slight tremor passed through her limbs as she spoke. To lift one's gaze toward the divine was a punishable sin; she had been taught that since she was old enough to walk. From the earliest moments of her memory, she had been given rules. Never go out after nightfall. Never lie. Always listen to her parents. Never look up without permission. Never question. Never want too much. And never this and never that.

And now, beneath the weight of her god's presence, Lyssena no longer knew what to do.

Erevos stood, and as he did, Lyssena felt the warmth return.

It wasn't the first time; it had happened before, once in her real room back in her own world, and again when she had first arrived in this place of living darkness. The temperature here was never truly cold, but never warm either; it hovered somewhere between, a place that had no season. But whenever Erevos drew near to her, something in the air changed, and the warmth blossomed in her chest.

"You may look at me," Erevos said, and Lyssena's heart began to pound so hard she thought it might tear through her ribs.

"How could I—?"

Had she misheard?

Had a god truly just *invited* her to raise her eyes?

"You could then," Erevos continued, "and you can now."

Her eyes widened so suddenly, so forcefully, that she thought, for a terrifying moment, this must be the end of her life. Surely no one was meant to survive such a sentence. Erevos had remembered. He had seen the moment she sinned when she first looked upon him.

And Lyssena broke.

Tears began to fall, one after another, slipping down her cheeks, past her chin, pooling at the base of her throat. Her whole body trembled with the weight of shame, of panic, of holy dread. She shook so violently that anyone watching might have thought her ill, or cursed, but she was not sick. She was terrified.

Terrified of punishment. Terrified of judgment. Terrified that she, a girl who had tried so hard to follow every rule she was ever given, had sinned in the one place she had longed to be safe.

She was sure that she was about to sink into the floor, fall into some pit, and *burn*.

"I'm so sorry," she sobbed, voice choked and desperate, "I beg you—please, please, do not take my life. I apologize—"

She cried and begged and shook in fear, her voice raw and her body going numb across her torso, and her fingertips ran cold. But still she didn't stop.

She *couldn't* stop.

Lyssena wept like the lost, pleaded like the condemned, and begged her god to spare her life.

Chapter Ten

The Language of Warmth

Erevos

His little songbird was shaking so violently that Erevos thought for a moment she must be ill.

Her cries were loud and fractured, rising and falling in waves so intense that he could barely make out the words, and the fact that he couldn't understand what she was saying did not please him. He had always listened closely and paid attention, and now, in the moment when she needed him most, her meaning was lost in the noise of her pain.

Since he couldn't ask her, Erevos concluded that he did not understand humans as well as he thought he did. For all his watching, for all his listening, there were still pieces missing.

And so, he decided not to speak.

He acted.

Erevos wrapped his arms around Lyssena gently, careful not to startle her further, and drew her into his embrace. At first, he lifted her too high—her feet dangled, and she flinched—

so he lowered her, perhaps too much. But after a moment, he found the balance, and she was nestled perfectly between his chest and arms, her head resting just beneath the hollow of his throat. As the seconds passed, her cries began to fade.

He did not understand why she wouldn't look at him.

She had looked before, when they first met. He had given her permission again. And yet, instead of meeting his gaze, she had burst into tears.

That reaction troubled him. Erevos felt . . . uneasy.

He didn't know the name for the feeling, didn't know if demons were even meant to feel it, but he recognized that something within him was different, and he knew that it wasn't right. Demons didn't feel much, after all. Nothing truly happened in their lives. There was only hunger, and the feeding of it. They were never bored, never entertained, never curious in the way mortals were. There had never been anything that stirred the quiet in him.

Until Lyssena.

And now, for the first time in all his years of watching her from the edges of her world, for all the time he had spent memorizing her movements and expressions and habits, he realized he was still far from understanding her.

He wanted to understand her. So much so, he had defied the norms of his own realm, bent the stillness of The Void into something livable and breathable for her. He had created a home where she would not die.

And now he saw that this, too, was only the beginning.

There was only one solution to the problem before him.

"Little songbird," he murmured, his voice as soft as shadow, as he pulled her closer, tucking her fully into the safety of his hold. He found he liked this more than he expected. He liked the feel of her heartbeat against his chest. He liked how small she was in his arms, how alive she felt.

She looked nothing like him, and that did not matter.

She was not like him in any way, and that mattered even less.

He found her . . . fascinating.

And the more he realized how much he didn't know, the more he felt something new take root inside him. *Eagerness.*

Erevos was eager to . . .

To what? What, exactly, was he eager for?

"May I ask two questions?" Lyssena's voice broke through his thoughts, and at last, her words reached him. He understood them.

Perhaps I am eager to understand.

"Was that the first question?" he asked, and Lyssena let out a small huff of laughter, barely more than a breath, but there. And Erevos felt something warm bloom within him, something that spread quietly through his chest.

Was that . . . joy?

"You may," he said, and turned toward the bed and remembered it wasn't one anymore. He couldn't sit with her there as he had hoped. But he wanted to try. He remembered watching her, many times before, curling into her blankets and folding herself into softness, and he had longed to feel what that was like. He had tried once, by himself, mimicking the shape of her rest, but it hadn't felt as it looked.

"This isn't . . . a goodbye hug, right?" Her voice came smaller again, threaded with shame.

And Erevos did not like that.

He did not want her voice to sound uncertain or brittle. He wanted to hear that tiny sound she made when she found him amusing, that small flicker of laughter when he tried to mimic the human custom of joking. He had learned about humor from watching mortals, seen how they twisted words and meanings into something clever, something that could bring warmth even to the coldest moments. And he found that he enjoyed it.

He wanted her to feel that again.

But Lyssena was afraid. He could feel it, so he would fix it.

He glanced at the bed and the chair, both reshaped by her will, both no longer serving to be seated on. He could have returned them to their original forms with a thought, but he didn't. Not without asking Lyssena first. She had commanded his shadows, shaped them for her own liking, and he would not take that from her without her permission.

He did not want to undo her choices.

And he did not want to shift the conversation away from what mattered, so he didn't ask. What mattered now was telling her the truth.

That with him, she was safe.

That with him, she would never die.

By the time Erevos finished wrestling with his own demons and was finally ready to answer his little songbird, he found that Lyssena had fallen asleep.

She had been so exhausted that her body had done what it must: surrendered to rest.

Once again, he had lost his chance to speak with her. The first time he had tried, there had been a man in the way—a man whose blood still was being scrubbed in her room. Then, Lyssena had needed food, and so Erevos had gone to find it for her. And now, when he had finally returned, when he was eager with thoughts to share and things to say and the warmth of emotion burning in his chest, she had fallen asleep in his arms.

He looked down at her gently curled form, her breath warm against his throat, and thought that she needed more space.

And the thought excited him.

This house he had made, this quiet home of shadow nestled deep within a forgotten cave in The Void, would grow. He would expand it for her, carve new spaces from darkness.

There were already a few rooms, empty ones, half-shaped, waiting for meaning. And in one of them Erevos now stood, while Lyssena slept within his arms.

He needed one arm to use, and so he adjusted her gently, shifting her weight until he held her in his left arm alone, her head nestled into the curve between his neck and shoulder.

He was aware of what he was—his body all shadow-bound muscle as if made from obsidian stone. He did not know if she was comfortable there, pressed against hardness and heat, but he hoped she was.

And he began to work.

Chapter Eleven

The Day of Too Many Teeth

Lyssena

A warm cup of tea in cold weather, a warm blanket after a long day, even the warm, fuzzy toe beans of the neighbor's cat, were the little wonders that made Lyssena feel at peace. Her eyes were still closed, and she snuggled deeper into her bed, letting the comfort stretch for a bit longer.

This bed was a bit hard, but so warm that she didn't mind it at all.

She felt a blanket brush through her hair. But her hair was long, and every stroke through her locks lingered, far too long for a blanket to be responsible.

Blankets didn't brush hair. Certainly not hers.

So she did what any clever, uncertain girl would do: she pretended to still be asleep.

Slowly, very carefully, she stretched her arms, letting her palms glide over the surface beneath her. It wasn't soft. It was warm but hard. Her hands moved gently, feeling along the shape, gliding up and down until she realized it wasn't a bed at all.

It was a body.

Far too big and far too solid to belong to any human she had ever known. And then Lyssena understood where she was. Or rather, *who* she was on.

She then remembered how hard she had cried, how certain she had been that she would die. And yet she hadn't; and that, perhaps, was the mercy of her god. Would an angry god spare the life of a lowly human? Would he cradle her so gently, stroke her hair with such care, and keep her wrapped in warmth if fury had been his intent?

"You are awake."

Lyssena's eyes flew open, and she nodded quickly. "I'm sorry, I—"

"You apologize a lot," Erevos said, his voice quiet, and Lyssena wasn't sure what to make of that.

She felt truly lost. She wanted so desperately to understand how she was meant to behave. In her village, everything had been simple, defined by rules and rituals, by expectations passed down like well-worn robes. She had known what to do, what to say, how to exist. Here, nothing was clear.

And yet, she was here, nestled in the lap of her god, held securely between his massive torso and muscled arms, and gods, it felt . . . good.

Her brothers had been strong too, built by years of labor in the fields, and she'd seen them often without tunics, wearing only trousers and boots as they worked. But this was entirely different.

It was only when she stirred slightly, when awareness trickled in like sunlight through leaves, that she realized she was sitting on the bare lap of a god, and the flush that spread across her face burned like fire. At twenty-three, she had never seen . . . *that* part of a body. And now she was practically on top of it.

And oh, how curious she was.

For a moment, she forgot the fear that had swallowed her whole, forgot that she was in the presence of a divine being she devoted herself to.

"Should I . . . " she began, the thought half-formed as her gaze drifted slowly down the sculpted lines of his abdomen, trailing even lower, unfocused and wide-eyed, "not apologize?" she mumbled, the words tumbling out more to herself than to him.

Just as her eyes neared the place her curiosity most longed to see, Erevos lifted his arm, and Lyssena's gaze shot upward.

Their eyes met.

And though her instincts urged her to look away, to retreat into herself like she always had before, Erevos did not let her.

He caught her jaw between his fingers, tilting her face up with a firmness that brooked no argument, forcing her gaze to remain on his.

"Am I not pleasing to your gaze?"

Lyssena absolutely did not expect so many teeth.

She hadn't seen his mouth before, or at least she hadn't known he had one at all, but now that she did, she was thoroughly, irrevocably stunned. Erevos's teeth were long and sharp and far too numerous, and Lyssena found herself speechless at the sight. If a creature like that—not Erevos, of course; not her god, never him, because she would never judge a divine being— but if a creature like *that* had come to her in the middle of the night, grinning down with that terrifying, toothy mouth, she would have preferred to drop dead on the spot and never—*ever* —wake up again.

His mouth stretched wider, unnervingly so, in something that seemed suspiciously like a . . . smile?

Goosebumps rippled across her entire body.

How could he ask her a question like that and then show her *that many teeth?* And worse, she couldn't lie, not even to save herself, because lying was a sin, and she *never* lied.

"What a . . . presentable mouth you have," Lyssena said slowly. So slowly, in fact, that she wondered if she had somehow forgotten how to speak at all. Her gaze flicked between his purple eyes and his frankly *very* white teeth. How did someone even brush two whole rows of those? The thought alone was overwhelming . . . and, in its own strange way, deeply impressive.

"Thank you," Erevos replied with a tone of amusement, and Lyssena felt, with some small sense of pride, that she had done well.

And then—without warning—he squished her cheeks.

"You are so soft, songbird."

Lyssena gasped, more out of surprise than protest. She hadn't expected that, but somehow, it wasn't the strangest part of her day. Instead, her thoughts snagged on the name he had used again, that gentle nickname he had said before she fell asleep, and now here it was again.

Also, she was very hungry.

Also, she was still alive.

Also, her god wanted her to *look* at him.

What a day.

Chapter Twelve

The Alchemy of Shadow and Spice

Erevos

Now Erevos knew that he had an impressive mouth. It was a fine compliment, one he accepted with pride.

He couldn't quite say the same for Lyssena, whose teeth were not nearly as formidable as his, but that didn't bother him. She would never need to hunt or tear flesh to feed herself; she would only need her teeth for chewing, and as far as he was aware, she was quite capable of that. He had, after all, watched her do it for many years.

Squishing Lyssena's face had been a small, indulgent joy, something he had wanted to do for longer than he realized. He hadn't expected it to happen so soon; it had simply occurred when he reached for her, when he held her chin to stop her from looking away again. But once it had happened, he found the experience incredibly pleasing.

He wondered when he might be able to squeeze more of her.

She had so many soft organs.

Lyssena had lush thighs and a lower belly that rounded out beneath her gown, and Erevos found himself deeply curious about those parts of her. He did not touch them because he wanted her to feel safe first, wanted her to know that she was not in danger with him. He didn't fully understand why the curiosity burned so strongly in him now. For years, when she was smaller, he had never once been distracted by the details of her body.

But now he had noticed the soft mounds on her chest, which he knew were for feeding offsprings in her kind, and the curve of her hips that gave way to a full, prominent behind, and how her arms had thickened, how even her face had taken on more fullness.

And all of it fascinated him.

He wanted to explore her.

Erevos rose, cradling Lyssena in his arms, and carried her toward the new table he had created. Atop it sat a bone-colored box, and beside it, two shadow-crafted plates, one resting over the other, covering the bread he had prepared for her.

He sat in the new chair and carefully settled Lyssena on his thigh.

She arched her back slightly, blinking the questions flickering behind her eyes without yet forming into words.

Erevos, however, was too eager to wait. He had longed to feed her for the whole time she was asleep, and now that the moment had come, he nearly wanted to place the entire piece in her mouth at once. But she had teeth for a reason, and he respected the form and function of her kind. He had worked too hard to ignore the process now, to disregard all the effort he had poured into creating the ingredients, shaping them from shadow, crafting them into something that could nourish her.

Erevos was a clever demon. For centuries, he had loved to

create and to mimic. He had learned that chairs were made from wood, and so he mimicked their consistency, carved the shape from shadow until it felt nearly identical to what he had observed in the human world.

Once, he had watched Lyssena as a child, spinning in a small gown, and when she left the room, he had studied the garment, then recreated it, stitch by stitch, from the essence of his shadows.

Over time, Erevos became skilled at mimicking nearly any non-living thing from the human realm.

When Lyssena ate her first apple, he had watched how it was grown, how it was picked, and he had mimicked the process, learning to craft apples from shadow.

Prepared food, however, had proven far more difficult.

His first attempt had been porridge. It had failed miserably.

But then came an idea so bold it delighted him. Instead of mimicking the final product, he would mimic the ingredients. One by one, he crafted them from shadow, and then he built a small flame, an imitation of fire, born from shadow laced with oxygen he had collected from the mortal realm. He had even forged a spark-stone, using more shadow twisted into the shape of what humans called flint.

The porridge had cooked. It had texture and warmth.

But it had no taste.

And that was a problem because Lyssena loved tasty things.

So Erevos made a bargain with Rolam, the demon who had everything, and from him, Erevos obtained spices. With them, he seasoned his shadow-born creations, coaxing flavor into form.

In that same way, this bread before them was created.

Lyssena looked at the two plates, her brows lifting in antici-pation, and turned to Erevos with a curious smile.

"I smell food," she said, rubbing her belly in small circles, and Erevos nodded, pleased beyond measure, gesturing for her to lift the plate that rested on top.

As Lyssena slowly reached forward, her fingertips brushing the edge, Erevos leaned in just a little closer, unable to restrain his eagerness. He had waited so long for this moment, and now it was finally happening.

"Is that bread?" she asked, the tips of her fingers already curling beneath the plate. "It smells so good!"

Erevos's mouth stretched wide, revealing the full, impressive range of his teeth. Humans smiled like this, he had learned, and Lyssena should know by now that this meant he was pleased.

But Lyssena did not look nearly as delighted as he felt, and instead of meeting his gaze, she turned her eyes back to the plate.

At last, she lifted the cover and revealed a large, thick loaf of bread, and inhaled deeply.

"Whoa," she breathed. Erevos did not know that word, but she said it with half a smile and a tone that rang with approval, so he decided it must mean *good*.

The loaf was dense and round, with a shape and scent nearly identical to the bread she used to buy at the bakery in her village, but this version was entirely black. Still, Lyssena didn't seem bothered by the color, and since she made no comment on it, Erevos did not ask.

"Is this for me?" she asked, looking up at him with wide, hopeful eyes, and Erevos nodded.

"But before you eat," he said, lifting his arm toward the bone-colored box and sliding it closer across the table, "you can add this."

Chapter Thirteen

Gods Don't Eat, They Watch

Lyssena

The last thing Lyssena expected was honey.

In a room made of darkness, seeing this pop of color made her chest tighten with homesickness, and she realized how much she missed her home. She didn't know if a day had already passed or not, as there were no windows to tell the passage of time, and she wouldn't dare ask her god, not when he had just spared her life and was now feeding her with a loaf of bread and honey.

She didn't know if it was right to miss the family that had sold her, fattened her, and cared for her only to hand her over to the highest bidder.

If her father had simply wanted her to marry a good man, he could have chosen any one of the villagers she knew. There were plenty of men of marriageable age. The baker's eldest son, for example, or the family living on the farm near their house, with seven children, four of whom were older than her, and the rest only slightly younger. These men weren't wealthy, but they weren't poor either.

But her father had chosen a cruel, wealthy knight instead, and hadn't even told her until it was already done.

So Lyssena buried all those false hopes deep within herself and decided, instead, to enjoy this strange and lovely bread that had been given to her.

"Would you join me?" she asked Erevos, tearing a piece of the soft loaf between her fingers. It was warm and puffy, practically sighing steam, and Lyssena couldn't wait to dip it into the honey and take the biggest bite.

"I made it for you, songbird. Eat," he said, and poured a generous stream of honey onto the plate.

Lyssena chose to take the first bite as it was, saving the dip for the next. And the taste, when it met her tongue, was divine.

The loaf was so soft, so cloudy and light in her mouth, that she let out a long hum as she chewed, eyes fluttering shut from the sheer joy of it.

It was, without question, the best bread she had ever eaten.

Lyssena thought of the many possible reasons Erevos would call her songbird, but she was far too busy tearing pieces from the massive loaf, chewing greedily, dipping them into the honey again and again, her mouth far too occupied and her hunger far too loud to dwell on the answer for long.

All Erevos did was add more honey to her plate, while his other hand held her waist with gentle pressure, keeping her balanced on his lap so she wouldn't fall.

Erevos was big—*so* big—that her feet dangled high above the ground, swinging freely. Lyssena wasn't considered short by human standards, not at all, but Erevos was so tall that even if she had been the tallest human alive, she still would have found her feet suspended in the air. Perhaps not as high as they were now, but dangling all the same.

As she finished chewing her very last bite, Erevos reached into the eggshell-colored box once more and retrieved a cup made of glass, and Lyssena's eyes widened with surprise.

She studied the beautiful cup in wonder, only to be further amazed when Erevos, with a flick of his fingers, opened a drawer to their right—one she hadn't even noticed was there—and another matching glass floated out and set itself gently on the table before them.

Then Erevos poured water into the cup and offered it to her.

Lyssena stood in a room that looked nothing like the first one she had turned into an armory. This one was far more elegant.

It looked like a room a princess might live in, if that princess adored the color black. In the center stood a massive bed with tall, carved posts that supported a roof draped in sheer, silky fabric, which fell softly from both sides like shadow-woven curtains. Beneath it lay a round carpet that looked as though it had been made from fur, plush, and deep under her feet. Against one wall stood an enormous closet, and beside it a table where she had just eaten her bread and honey, paired with a single chair, both perfectly matched in design and material.

Surprisingly, everything was coordinated, and, of course, it was all black. Everything here, too, was made from shadow.

It looked like the kind of room the wealthiest daughter in the world might own, one who had never been denied a thing in her life, and Lyssena stood on that thick, fur-like carpet and blinked.

"I can't even believe I'd ever see a place like that," she

murmured to herself while grabbing the chair and moving it near the drawers that Erevos had summoned water from.

The chair was sturdy enough to support Erevos's weight, and Lyssena was feeling brave, so she climbed onto it and reached for the top drawer. She had to rise onto her toes to reach it, stretching just enough to grab the handle, but her curiosity was stronger than her caution, and she needed to know what else might be hidden inside.

Lyssena found a collection of beautiful, dark glass plates, cups, and spoons. *Next time*, she thought with a small smile, *I could eat honey with a spoon*, if her god would give her more. From the look he had given her earlier, she had a strong feeling that he just might. Erevos had looked as though he enjoyed her eating, almost as if *he* were the one tasting the food, and Lyssena couldn't help but wonder what gods ate.

If they ate anything at all.

There were so many questions bubbling inside her, questions she longed to ask, and she was only waiting for the right moment to let them out. But what that moment would look like, or how she would recognize it, she simply didn't know.

She knew she could look at him now, and that he was kind, and for now, that felt like enough.

But eventually, sooner or later, Lyssena knew she would get bored if she was left to do nothing; she also knew that soon, she would need to relieve herself, and she had no idea where or how she was supposed to do that in a place like this—shadows and all.

She wondered if there were other humans in this place, tucked into homes by other gods like hers. If this were something that gods did, each choosing a human to care for in their own strange way.

She wondered so much, and still couldn't ask. But she would.

When the time was right.

Erevos had said he would be right back, and Lyssena decided that, since her god had been nothing but kind to her so far, maybe she was allowed to peek around and take a closer look at what this strange, beautiful space had to offer.

So she did.

And she began with a deep breath.

Chapter Fourteen

Whispers Between Walls

Lyssena

This was a whole house made of shadows.

So much so, it made Lyssena wonder whether gods lived like humans, whether they, too, needed kitchens and bedrooms and halls and quiet spaces to exist in. Besides her two rooms, it had a kitchen that looked almost exactly like the one in her home and a hallway. Even a living room, though it had no furniture at all.

Lyssena walked down the long corridor, which was far simpler than the detailed, ornate rooms she had explored so far. It had only smooth walls on either side and a flat floor beneath her feet: all of it, of course, made from shadow.

Every room she had seen so far was lit by the same soft gray orb that floated near the ceiling, but here, in the hallway, there was no light at all.

Lyssena felt a prickle of unease as she moved through the darkness, the silence existing all around her, but she was feeling brave today, and far too curious to sit quietly in her room doing nothing.

With one hand resting on the wall to guide her and the other gripping her gown, she kept walking. She had been walking for several minutes and still hadn't found the end of the hall. Occasionally, her hand would brush over a raised section of the wall—like bricks stacked atop one another—but strangely, not the entire wall was made this way; just patches, here and there, as if something were half-formed, or still growing.

To calm herself, Lyssena began to hum a soft melody, one she remembered from the traveling minstrels who would visit her village to entertain the people during the harvest months. She had never been allowed to join the adult dances, as she was unmarried, but sometimes the musicians would orchestrate little dances just for the younger girls, and then she was allowed to join.

"Huuuuuuman?"

Lyssena's heart dropped straight into her stomach.

That same voice slithered through the air around her, and she looked frantically to both sides, eyes wide, hands beginning to tremble very hard.

"Oh, you are . . . I can feel your heart beating."

With a cry that tore from her throat, Lyssena darted forward, eyes squeezed shut, screaming as she ran, breath leaving her lungs in ragged bursts until she had no air left at all.

"Lyssen—"

"Ah!" Lyssena cried out just as she slammed into something solid, and when she opened her eyes, she realized it was Erevos.

"I . . . I . . . " she stammered, breathless and struggling to form even a single sentence as her chest rose and fell rapidly. Erevos moved his head in that inhuman way of his and placed his massive hand gently atop Lyssena's head.

She instinctively lowered her gaze, but then caught herself, remembering that she was allowed to look at him now—that he had told her so—and suddenly she needed the reassurance of his presence more than ever. She needed to meet his eyes and know that everything was alright.

Erevos moved his hand over her head slowly, as if petting a cat, then reached down to take her hand in his and turned around without a word.

Lyssena hadn't even noticed there was an entrance behind him, hadn't seen the space open there like a waiting mouth, so she simply followed, still trembling, still trying to slow her breathing and pull herself back together.

This room was unlike the others she had seen so far.

Every breath she took echoed against the walls, and the walls themselves didn't look like the rest of the house. They were jagged and uneven, textured like natural stone.

It looked like a cave. A massive, black cave.

"What made you scream?" Erevos asked, his voice echoed around the cave as he stopped just before a dark pool. It looked like water, but moved and shimmered like ink.

With one hand pressed against her chest, Lyssena lifted her eyes to him and swallowed the saliva that had gathered under her tongue.

"I heard . . . a voice," she said at last.

Lyssena did not want her god to leave her alone. Not to chase down the voice, not to investigate the unknown. And yet, just as much, she did not want him to think she was useless, or worse . . . that she had brought trouble with her.

"Did the voice say anything?" Erevos asked, lowering himself down to sit on his heels.

In that position, Lyssena was, for once, slightly taller than him. And that made her . . .

What *did* that make her?

A god had lowered himself before her, while she stood tall and looked him in the eyes.

Lyssena decided, then and there, that perhaps everything she had known before meeting Erevos no longer mattered. In this place, with this god, it was becoming clearer and clearer that the rules she had lived by simply did not apply.

"Will I ever go home?" she asked. It slipped from her lips before she could stop it, and Erevos arched his back slightly in reaction, as though he, too, did not expect that to come out of her mouth.

"Is that what the voice asked you?"

Lyssena felt foolish. A silly, overwhelmed girl, full of questions she still didn't know how to ask, so consumed by thoughts and curiosity that she had entirely lost the thread of their conversation. She didn't want her god to think she was scattered or weak, and certainly not foolish.

All she truly wanted, right now, was to sit him down and ask him *everything* from what he meant by calling her songbird, to what her purpose was here, and why he had chosen her.

She shook her head and murmured, "The voice said it knew I'm a human."

At that, Erevos nodded once, slowly, and then stood again, stretching to his full, towering height. Lyssena assumed that he would deal with the matter now—that he would leave her behind to take care of whatever danger lurked—but instead, he turned toward the inky black pool.

"Would you like to bathe?" he asked.

Would she like to bathe? In an unfamiliar place, in water as black as a raven's wing, with a god standing nearby? Would he simply stay and watch her?

No, he would probably leave her to it, she reasoned, likely going off to investigate the strange voice while she cleaned herself.

So Lyssena nodded.

Both the god and Lyssena stood in silence, eyes locked, saying nothing.

Lyssena couldn't understand why he wasn't leaving. Wasn't he going to investigate the voice, or give her some privacy? And Erevos, for his part, seemed to be . . . waiting?

But waiting for *what*?

"I'm sorry—" she began, just as—

"Why aren't y—" he started to say at the same time.

What a tragedy it was that neither of them finished their sentence. Their words crashing into each other mid-air and falling to the ground between them.

Lyssena cleared her throat, flustered, and gestured for Erevos to continue, but instead of speaking, he simply crossed the space between them in two long strides and lifted her effortlessly into his arms.

A small, startled whimper escaped her lips as she clutched at his shoulders, her breath catching, her heart thundering so loudly in her chest that she was certain he could hear it echoing against the walls of this dark cave.

Chapter Fifteen

What Songbirds Sing

Erevos

Erevos assumed that his little songbird was afraid to be alone. And while that was true, it wasn't the whole truth. Lyssena was afraid of the voice she had heard, which was what had startled her so deeply when he returned, and what still unsettled her even now.

This was not good.

His suspicions had been confirmed. There *was* a demon who knew he had a human, and that knowledge alone made Erevos tighten his fists on Lyssena's back.

He decided that he would kill that demon, but not now, while Lyssena was scared and tucked close to his chest. He would wait until she was asleep, safe and unaware, and then he would do what must be done.

For now, he would bathe her, because it seemed she did not wish to do it on her own. Erevos had seen her many times walk into the bathing room in the human realm, always dressed when she entered, and dressed again when she left. He did not understand why humans would bathe in their clothes, but then there were many human habits he had never fully understood and never much cared to question.

Perhaps she undressed within, bathed, and then dressed again in clean clothing, but why bring the clean garments into the bathing space? That remained a mystery to him, one of many.

Either way, his Lyssena had not undressed now, and that made the situation more complicated than it needed to be. He thought she understood by now that he only wanted to care for her, to keep her safe, to provide her with comfort in every way he knew how.

Lyssena fascinated him beyond meaning; her devotion, her soul, the very *essence* of her being consumed his thoughts like nothing else ever had. And she made him feel heat—a strange, burning warmth that stirred beneath his skin—just like she did now, nestled once more in his arms, allowing herself to be held.

Much like he was, Lyssena was a curious creature. She stared at the pool of water with such intensity, her brows drawn tightly together, that Erevos felt a growing eagerness to ease her into it and bathe her.

They were different and so much alike.

So he stepped toward the edge, waded into the dark water, and lowered both himself and Lyssena until he was seated fully within it, the surface rising to his ribs while she remained cradled in his arms.

For some reason, Lyssena's eyes grew wider with every inch he lowered them, her gaze darting around the room, her breath quickening with each passing second.

The water was warm and inviting, so much so that even a demon like Erevos, emotionless by nature and untouched by most sensations, found himself feeling something close to comfort. He had studied humans bathing in hot springs, observed the steam and the satisfaction on their faces, and had taken it upon himself to learn what made the water stay warm —how it worked, how it felt.

And once he understood, he had recreated it here, in their home, mimicking everything down to the minerals and heat. It had taken a long time to perfect; it wasn't easy to make water from shadow, but he had managed it, as he always did, because Erevos was, quite simply, a very intelligent demon.

"Is the water too hot?" he asked his little songbird, noting the way she now shielded her chest with her arms, and that was when he realized that the white gown she wore had turned sheer where the fabric touched the water.

Erevos hummed thoughtfully.

"No, the water . . . is fine. Thank you. Just . . . " Lyssena mumbled, voice small and tight, and Erevos, wanting her to feel more confident, decided to do what had comforted her before. He placed her on his lap just like he had when she'd eaten, holding her thigh gently, exactly as he had done then. Perhaps familiarity would soothe her.

Well, it did *not*.

The moment he had a full view of her, now pressed lightly against him and lit by the dim light above the pool, Lyssena shrieked.

Perhaps his human was still uncertain, and of course, she would be. How foolish of Erevos to think Lyssena could feel entirely comfortable without even having a proper conversation first. She had spent her time here afraid, or asleep, or eating, barely getting to know him at all.

Conversation was important.

He wanted to understand her, but he also wanted to *be* understood, and more than anything, he wanted to hear the questions she still hadn't asked.

So he began with one of his own.

"You wanted to ask me, Lyssena," he said, his gaze shifting slowly between her eyes.

Erevos did not fully understand what the word *beautiful* meant. He had heard humans use it to describe flowers, sunsets, even one another. But he did understand the idea of a *beautiful soul*, and Lyssena's was just that. Perhaps, if her soul was beautiful, then *she* was beautiful too. "What was your question before?"

Lyssena went still.

"Oh," she breathed, the sound soft and uncertain as her gaze flicked upward, first toward the cave ceiling, then toward the dim gray orb that floated above them. "You've called me a songbird," she said slowly. "Why?"

Erevos reached with his free hand to take hers, small and damp from the water, as she sat on his thigh, no longer as tense as before.

"A songbird in your world," he began, feeling the gentle heat that spread from the base of his palm where their skin touched, "is a creature caged . . . yet taken care of, Lyssena."

His claws traced lightly over her fingers, making her heart flutter wildly inside her chest.

Erevos did not have eyes like hers—no irises, no pupils, no colors—but the dark expanse of purple where his gaze lived was locked onto her heartbeat, watching how it thumped in her chest, how it pulsed in her throat, how it flickered against the wrist he now held so delicately in his large, shadow-dark hand, his black skin seeming to swallow hers whole.

"Am I . . . in a cage now too?" she asked, and her words made Erevos pause.

Was she?

Had he simply exchanged one prison for another, even if this one was wrapped in comfort and shadows and care? How different was her life now, truly, now that she was with him?

She was being fed—she was never hungry then. She had a space of her own—again, she had one in there as well. It hadn't even been a full day yet, and Erevos had so much planned for his little songbird, so many ideas and spaces and comforts he wanted to build for her.

But how could he ever claim she was *free* if she could not do as she pleased?

In the human world, she had been able to step outside, and that particular truth concerned him deeply. Here, in The Void, there was no oxygen, no air for her lungs to draw in, no atmosphere in which she could survive.

And that was a very big problem if Erevos wanted Lyssena to *truly* be as she wished. To thrive, not merely survive. He would need to find a solution.

And then he did.

Oh, what a glorious solution he had in mind. So clever, so perfect, that it made his mouth curl into a slow, widening grin.

Chapter Sixteen

The Pool of Ink and Echoes

Lyssena

What did it mean when you asked a god whether you were in a cage and he grinned?

Lyssena was absolutely horrified by that reaction. She had agreed to go with him, but now, seeing that grin stretch across his face, she was suddenly very concerned for her safety.

Was this still better than marrying Kaan?

She didn't know the answer to that, and so, instead of dwelling on it, she blinked slowly, took a long breath, and tried to calm herself down.

"I would always do as you wish, greatest Erevos," she whispered, swallowing down the dread that had begun to rise in her throat.

She was no longer thinking about how soaked her gown had become, how the dark ink-water clung to the fabric and made it translucent all the way up to her chest, until Erevos said: "Do not move."

She didn't.

She froze, staring at him with wide eyes, waiting silently for whatever would come next.

His hand moved slowly from her wrist, down the arch of her arm, up to her shoulder, and the motion made Lyssena gulp again, her breath catching as she followed the path of his fingers.

Then his hand rose to cup her cheek, his palm so large it covered half her face and some of her scalp. Erevos began to trace the outline of her face, circling it slowly.

What for? She didn't know, and truthfully, she was far too distracted to ask.

She was too focused on counting the number of times her heart pounded in her ears, too wrapped up in the sensation of his touch as his fingers drifted downward, gliding along her neck, circling her throat with the same slowness.

He didn't press, he didn't choke or threaten, and yet he was so focused, so utterly absorbed in what he did, that it truly seemed like he was doing something far beyond simply wanting to kill her.

Lyssena realized she had been foolish to think he might kill her because Erevos wasn't preparing to harm her; he was *studying* her.

She felt his arm wrap securely around her waist, drawing her closer until her breasts pressed against the hardness of his chest, the soft curves of her body yielding against his unmoving form. His massive, stone-like abs compressed against her soft belly, and for a long, quiet moment, Erevos looked at her, and she looked right back at him.

That was when she noticed that he didn't breathe.

His chest did not rise or fall, did not move at all. She, however, was breathing fast and shallow, and every exhale brushed against his skin, as though her breath were painting warmth onto him.

Her body was growing hotter by the second, and Erevos suddenly became still. Their position made her tilt her head up to look at him, her chin raised because of how tall he was, and how close they were now. So close that her hair fell behind her like a dark curtain, damp and trailing down the length of her back.

She couldn't tell where he was looking—at her eyes, her nose, maybe even her mouth. His gaze was impossible to read without irises or even pupils, only those endless purple orbs glowing faintly in the cave's dim light.

But he was staring.

And then he was touching her face again.

Not her cheek this time. His claw traced slowly across her brow, then down the bridge of her nose, and Lyssena could feel the heat rising to her face, turning her skin red not just from the warmth radiating from Erevos but from her own overwhelming embarrassment.

No one had ever touched her like this.

No one had *ever* looked at her like this.

He was studying her with such intensity that she couldn't look away. The soft sound of water droplets falling echoed through the cave, and beyond that faint rhythm, the only other sounds were her breathing . . . and her pounding heart.

When Erevos's claw reached her lips, he slowed. So much so that it barely hovered above the curve of her mouth, and Lyssena forgot how to breathe altogether.

More than that, she felt a strange, building heat gathering between her legs.

Erevos pulled back slightly, his claw no longer brushing her lip.

"What's that?" he asked, and Lyssena squirmed in response.

What could she possibly tell her god? That his touch made her excited? That every movement of his hand, every inch of his closeness, set her skin aflame with a heat she had never known before?

She couldn't help herself. He was tall and muscular and so impossibly gentle. She couldn't deny those things, not even to herself.

"I . . . " she murmured, before letting out a noise so high-pitched and sudden that even Erevos flinched.

Lyssena immediately glued herself to his chest, hiding from the gaze of her god, tucking herself into the dark safety of his neck and shoulder.

Was it a sin to feel aroused in the presence of a god? Had any god ever touched a human like that before?

She covered her face with her hands, heat flooding her cheeks, and buried herself deeper beneath Erevos's chin.

"I want to wash up. Please," she said, her voice muffled against her palms.

She couldn't believe she was attracted to a god.

Lyssena felt a deep vibration rumble through Erevos's chest. Was it a hum? A growl? Did gods even growl?

"Of course, Lyssena. But you cannot be truly clean if you have clothes on," he said, his voice low as his claws glided slowly through her hair.

"I know . . . " she whispered against his neck, her words barely audible, just as she felt her gown begin to lift from her skin.

Her god had decided to undress her.

She couldn't take it seriously, not when Erevos was a god and could do anything he pleased, not when she was the one trembling and flustered, the one making everything so difficult with her tangled thoughts and human shame.

And so Lyssena made a decision to stop huffing and puffing against her own nerves and simply wash herself.

She sat upright, raising her arms above her head as Erevos carefully lifted her now completely soaked gown. She had nothing to cover her breasts, but at least her cunt remained shielded by the linen that clung to her thighs. Still, as the fabric rose inch by inch, she felt every thread like a part of her being peeled from her skin, and when the wet cloth finally slid over her nipples, she realized how hard they had become, how unprepared she was for this flood of sensations overtaking her body.

"Your scent is very sweet, Lyssena," Erevos murmured, his voice thoughtful, curious, as if he were making a divine observation. "I wonder why it has changed."

By the time he finished speaking, her gown was gone, folded neatly and placed on a cave floor, and his hand—his large, clawed, shadow-dark hand—was cupping water to pour over her head.

The warmth flowed down her scalp, her neck, her back, and Lyssena exhaled slowly, letting the sensation anchor her. But she remained painfully aware that she was bare before him.

And yet, Erevos didn't seem to mind her nudity at all. He didn't gawk, didn't leer; he simply watched her with the same calmness he always did, as if her being unclothed was just another form of truth.

That should have comforted her, and perhaps it did, but something inside her wilted, too. Was it disappointment?

Well, what had she expected? For a god to be aroused by a

mortal girl? That was the question she should have been asking, instead of fretting over imagined slights.

Perhaps it was for the best.

Lyssena dipped her hands into the warm pool, scooped water into her palms, and began washing.

Chapter Seventeen

A Mask to See the Truth

Erevos

His songbird's scent still lingered in Erevos's mind as he shaped his shadows into the delicate face of a bird. A songbird, to be exact.

He heard Lyssena's footsteps as she left her old bedroom and made her way through the quiet hallway. When she stepped into what was now her new room—the one where Erevos stood—she tilted her head and asked, "How do I look?" swaying her hips from side to side.

The shadowy gown he had crafted for her hugged her form well, but Erevos believed that anything would suit her. Everything she wore in the human realm had looked good, had enhanced the curve of her body, the softness in her shape, the warmth of her skin.

"It suits you well," he said, setting the half-formed mask on the table beside him. "Would you want shoes?"

At that, Lyssena nodded, and Erevos began walking toward her.

There was a strange feeling moving through him as he did, something unfamiliar and unnameable, something he could not quite grasp or pin down.

Lyssena's expression had changed, too. She no longer looked at him with fear, not like before, and that in itself made him pause. If not fear . . . then what was it?

He didn't know.

Lowering himself to his heels before her, Erevos extended one hand so she could place her foot in it. She hesitated and then gently set her foot into his palm.

Erevos looked at her toes. They were small, different from his. Well, he didn't exactly have toes, not in the way humans did, but he also didn't have hair, and that was another difference, one of many, all of which he had started to notice with increasing fascination.

Placing his other hand over her foot, he summoned his shadows and wrapped them around her heel, shaping them forward to curl over her toes. He created a shoe that was firm yet soft, crafted with a cushioning lace along the sole so that she would feel no bumps or sharp edges as she walked.

Then he repeated the same process for her other foot, and when he finished, Lyssena stood with a new pair of shoes and entirely her own.

"Thank you so much, greatest," Lyssena said with a smile, and Erevos felt that heat again. The same strange warmth that had begun to coil in his chest refused to leave.

For some reason, he found himself wanting to embrace her, to feel her close again.

It confused him . . . this new sensation.

He had been fascinated by Lyssena for so many years. He watched her, studied her, knew her as one might know a rare and ancient song, but he had never felt this warmth before, this need to be near.

"Of course," he replied, rubbing his chest with one clawed hand, as if the act might somehow still the sensation within.

Erevos turned back toward the table, where the unfinished mask waited for him, and behind him, Lyssena walked in her new shoes toward the chair, her steps light and curious. She sat down, leaned her elbows onto the shadowy table, and peered at the strange object he was crafting.

"What's that?" she asked, watching as Erevos added a slender, curved beak to the forming face of what would soon become a songbird's head.

"A mask with oxygen," he answered, shaping the piece with both hands. "I want you to be able to walk outside."

He continued his work, adding the eyes now, though this part was difficult, more complicated than it seemed.

He couldn't leave the eyes hollow, for the air in The Void could harm Lyssena's vision. But he couldn't make them opaque either; if the mask were completely black, she would not see at all.

So Erevos created the thinnest surface of shadow, a film so fine it would tint the world in a darker shade but still allow her to see through it. He shaped it slowly, carefully, and Lyssena watched him all the while, then asked, "Where are we? What is this place?"

He had wanted to explain everything to her when they bathed, though he was too distracted with everything that was happening there, and he simply forgot.

Erevos had never forgotten anything, never felt this warmth in his chest, never been drawn like that to anyone and anything. And yet now, he was.

"In the world," Erevos began, "there are many dimensions." He wasn't sure she would fully understand, as humans had not yet discovered the truth of such things, but he tried anyway. "In one of them, your kind lives. And in others . . . imagine it as layers of a world stacked one atop another. In one of those layers, we exist."

"Gods?" Lyssena asked, propping herself up on one elbow, her brows drawn with thought.

"Gods do not exist, Lyssena," Erevos said calmly. "A god is a concept created by humans to ease their souls when the time is hard. And as it evolved, it became a tool of control."

"How come? There are temples and prayers and—"

"What *is* a god?" he asked, and Lyssena went quiet.

After Lyssena ate her bowl of porridge sweetened with honey, she curled into her new bed. It was a true princess bed, in every sense of the word, for Erevos had shaped it in the likeness of one he had once seen beneath a real princess in the human realm, with silken drapes that shimmered like moonlight, if the moon was black, and carvings that swirled like wind over frozen glass.

He pulled the thick, weighty blanket up to her shoulders, its texture soft as velvet and warm as breath, then stood silently beside her, watching the slow rise and fall of her chest before he turned, stepped back, and closed the door behind him with a soundless sweep of shadow.

It was time to kill a demon.

Without hesitation, Erevos dissolved into smoke and shadow, his form unwinding into inky ribbons that slithered into the thick walls of the home he had made, and when he emerged once more beyond their protective edge, he reformed in silence, inhaling deeply, trying to trace the lingering scent of the one who had dared approach what was his.

Demons did not have strong scents. They usually smelled like the places they haunted—funerals, fire, stone, or rot—and Erevos, too, once bore that blank, hollow smell of emptiness.

But now, he smelled of Lyssena, of her skin, of her warmth, of the honey she had eaten and the soft wet minerals of the hot spring where he had held her. For a reason he could not explain, that scent pleased him in a way that was both unfamiliar and deeply satisfying.

Just as it pleased him that Lyssena was beginning to put together the pieces of the human system, that she was starting to question the foundation of the world she had come from, and what she had been told to believe.

She still thought he was a god, but not entirely; she was finally hesitating.

He wanted her to understand, but not through fear or doctrine, not through the human ways of sermons and submission. He wanted her to discover the truth for herself, to unearth it slowly like one might uncover buried light beneath layers of dust and time, and he would be there to guide her.

As he moved, Erevos rounded the high, jagged walls carved from shadow, his gaze scanning the endless paths of the cave system he had claimed for his own, the air around him thick with the silence of undisturbed dark.

So far, there was nothing unusual.

But when he reached the mouth of the outer cave, something caught his eye—a thin streak of red slashed across the stone.

A trace of blood.

And demons, as he well knew, did not bleed.

Chapter Eighteen

Blood Where There Should Be None

Erevos

E revos followed the scent of blood flooding his senses with a metallic tang that clung to the inside of his throat. It smelled like the armor worn by knights in the human realm, like coins rubbed together between anxious fingers, like pots and trays warmed by fire. These were familiar metals, but strange here, for such things did not belong in The Void, had no place in its vast, airless silence.

And that alone made the scent dangerous.

He did not know what he would find at the end of it, only that it was foul and wrong, and he had to see. So he went.

He passed through the crooked trees, their limbs like hands reaching into the ever-dark, and pushed through bushes with leaves as thin as ash. He crossed stones as smooth as bone and rivers that did not flow with water but with shadow made thick and slow, like ink drawn through silk.

And still the scent pulled him forward.

It led him to a narrow mouth of another cave, one among

many scattered across The Void, but this one reeked more than the others, reeked of wet iron and rotting heat, reeked of something fresh.

He walked inside, and the stillness changed around him, growing heavier and damper.

Erevos began to hear something spilling.

Something tearing, wet, and uneven.

Something quickening like frantic steps or breath or both.

And then something breaking.

The deeper he walked, the stronger the scent became, until finally, in the center of the cave, perched atop a stone slick with something dark, he saw a demon. Low and hunched, sitting still in the middle of the cave.

"Erevos," said the demon, its voice low and wet.

Erevos did not know his name, but he had seen this one lurking in the far corners of The Void before. Now, he feasted.

The demon crouched over the carcass of a deer. It was dead, rotting, alien to this place, for no such creature existed in The Void, and it tore into its flesh with a hunger that seemed unnatural for a creature like him.

Bones, slick with gore, clattered to the floor and rested against his knees, and blood . . . thick, dark blood poured freely down his chest, soaking into the slick sheen of his black skin, coating the ridges of his rib cage and slithering down to something Erevos could barely comprehend.

An organ, hard and pulsing, jutted grotesquely from between the demon's legs, and he was stroking it, his blood-slicked hand moving faster and faster, pumping with a rhythm.

The demon breathed hard through his jagged teeth, each one glistening red, and Erevos could only stare.

He had never seen a demon behave like this. Never seen one bring an animal from the human realm into The Void, never seen one consume flesh at all.

Demons fed on emotions—fear, lust, pain, joy—but this one was consuming meat.

His hand moved faster, and the blood cascading down its throat with saliva and filth, a perverse waterfall of heat and hunger.

"Your human," the demon rasped, those two words emerging in a high, fractured whine. His voice cracked under the weight of his desire, and that was when Erevos felt *anger*.

Hot, seething, primal anger—something he had never known—flared through his core, and it spilled out of him in a loud snarl, so sharp and violent it echoed like thunder across the cave walls.

This was the demon who had frightened Lyssena. This was the thing defiling flesh, drooling sickness, stroking himself with blood while whispering about Erevos's little songbird. This was the one he had to destroy.

"You always feed on so many humans . . . give me the girl," the demon rasped, his breath quickening, his hand a blur as he stroked himself. "I want to fuck her while I suck her cries of pleasure and drink from her cunt," he gasped, voice slipping into a panting rhythm that made Erevos's fists curl tighter. "And when I'm done—" he squeezed the tip of his organ until liquid bubbled at the slit, "—I'll consume her flesh."

The demon let out a guttural sound of pure pleasure, and Erevos did not wait.

With a single command, his shadows surged forward like blackened tendrils, and they tore the demon's length apart, ripping it down the middle.

Erevos clenched his fists as a heat like molten stone erupted inside his chest—true, bubbling rage that poured through him like it had always been waiting there, dormant until now.

He did not know he was capable of this kind of fury, just as he hadn't known he could feel warmth. But Lyssena had made him feel.

Lyssena was his.

Mine.

And now, he understood it. His little songbird had stirred something even demons were not meant to feel.

"Erev . . . os," the demon growled, voice strangled and wet with agony, and for a moment Erevos thought he heard real, true pain, the kind that demons were never supposed to feel.

That wasn't right.

Demons didn't feel pain.

Demons couldn't die the way mortals did, but they could be unmade, could be erased, destroyed, and vanish from the face of The Void, and Erevos intended to do just that.

But before he consumed the broken creature before him, he asked, "Why do you do this?"

As Erevos's shadows slithered around his throat, choking him, coiling tighter like serpents made of smoke and wrath, the demon let out a low, rattling sound and spoke.

"Aren't you bored?" he hissed, his voice both broken and amused. "Don't you want to feel?"

Erevos could hardly believe what he just heard.

"Come on," the demon coughed, stretching his cracked mouth wider and wider, splitting his cheeks with the motion, revealing far too many teeth. "You want to live an empty life? Oh . . . oh, you *can* feel."

Those were the last words he ever spoke.

Because Erevos consumed him whole.

After standing in the cave for quite some time, surrounded by the lingering stench of blood and decay, Erevos made a decision to burn everything inside.

If other demons came and fed on the remains, if they drew power or pleasure from what had happened here, it could only lead to ruin.

So Erevos summoned his shadows, and they coiled through the cave like smoke made of fire, and they consumed the filth.

They licked over the blood-soaked stone, dissolved the broken bones, devoured the rotting carcass of the deer, and swallowed the air itself until the cave was nothing but heat, silence, and ash.

Only Erevos could burn with shadow. It was a skill as rare as it was precise.

He watched as the last remnants of the foul scene crumbled into nothing, and then he stood in silence again.

Erevos was a smart demon. He was observant and curious. He knew he was not like most of his kind, and he had known it for a long time.

Where others did not care, he did.

Where others lived in endless cycles of dull hunger and forgotten centuries, he watched and learned. And it displeased him, deeply, that this grotesque, corrupted demon reminded him . . . of himself.

But he could not lie to himself; he enjoyed *feeling*.

He enjoyed seeing Lyssena eat honey with soft sounds of satisfaction; he enjoyed the way her laughter spilled from her throat like a melody only he was meant to hear.

He had known for some time that he could *enjoy* things as he had studied pleasure, understood satisfaction, but he hadn't realized until recently that he could actually *feel*.

Not just contentment.

Joy.

He had felt it the moment Lyssena laughed at the joke he made, the moment she tasted the honey he offered with her eyes shining bright. It was a strange, fluttering warmth in his chest that refused to leave.

He wanted to feel it again.

And again.

He wanted to learn how to make her happy, how to create moments like that not only for her, but with her.

He wanted to feel together with his songbird.

Chapter Nineteen

The Painter's Muse

Lyssena

Lyssena woke up warmer than usual, cocooned in her new, impossibly soft bed, wrapped in layers of luxurious blankets and surrounded by an indulgent abundance of pillows that cradled her on all sides like a nest built for royalty.

It was everything she could have asked for, waking up like a true princess, swaddled in comfort, her body sinking slightly into the plush mattress.

The fact that everything around her was black—the sheets, the curtains, the soft shimmer of shadow curling at the corners of the room—didn't bother her in the slightest.

If anything, it made her feel . . . special.

She was a splash of color, a living contrast in a place carved entirely from shadow, and somehow that made her feel more seen, more alive.

She let her thoughts drift, wondering what her family might think if they saw her now, saw her lying in luxury, protected and cared for, watched over by a being who had given her more than they ever had.

But they didn't deserve Erevos's kindness.

A god—whether he claimed to be one or not—so merciful and strange and gentle, would never waste his grace on those who had betrayed her, who had judged and discarded her in the name of appearances and greed.

Perhaps she was greedy, too. And yet . . . that didn't bother her.

There was something strange blooming inside her, a sense of freedom that wasn't about distance or location, but about the ability to act, to think, to speak, to look Erevos in the eyes and not feel shame.

It was a freedom that made her feel like she could breathe for the first time.

No one was telling her to rise early, to scrub the floors or polish the furniture until her fingers ached.

Though she admitted to herself that there were times she enjoyed cleaning, especially when she was angry.

She loved muttering to herself, venting under her breath as she dusted the corners of rooms no one else would bother to notice.

But now, as she blinked her eyes open fully, that familiar, comforting ritual was replaced by her god.

Erevos was lying beside her.

It was the first time she had ever seen him in a truly resting position, his long body still and strangely peaceful against the dark of the bedding, and something about the sight filled her with a gentle warmth that had nothing to do with the blankets.

It felt . . . nice.

It felt domestic, and Lyssena loved domesticity.

"You're awake," Erevos said, his voice deep and manly, and

Lyssena turned on her side to face him, her hair falling in a soft wave over her face.

He was watching her with those dark, unblinking eyes—hard to read, as always, like purple glass reflecting a world she couldn't see—and for some reason, Erevos looked . . . larger than usual.

Maybe it was the angle. Maybe it was the strangeness of seeing him reclined. The bed was enormous, but Erevos, lying still and massive in its side, seemed almost larger than the space allowed.

"We say good morning," she said with a sleepy smile, then added, "Good morning."

"Good morning," Erevos repeated, his wide mouth stretching into a grin that revealed far too many teeth once again, and though she was getting better at seeing them, she still wasn't entirely used to the way they gleamed in the low light.

She cleared her throat, her smile faltering just a little. "Lots of impressive teeth."

"I know," he replied, and his grin only widened, as if he took pride in her observation.

He lay propped on one muscular arm, his dark body coiled like a great feline at rest, and when Lyssena let her gaze drift lower, she noticed—quite suddenly—that one of his legs was crossed over the other, his knee slightly raised, and his foot hanging loose in the most casual, peculiar way.

She blinked.

And then she laughed.

Where on Earth had he picked up that pose? She would never have imagined Erevos lounging like that, like a bored aristocrat or an over-posed statue.

Erevos followed her gaze with curiosity and asked, "What amuses you, songbird?"

But Lyssena was already rolling onto her back, clutching her sides as she laughed even harder, breathless with delight.

"You," she gasped between fits of laughter, "You're lying like . . . like a painter's model! From the big cities!"

It was true. She'd seen those kinds of paintings sold in the market stalls of her village, smuggled from the cities and kept in leather-bound folios, whispered about behind hands.

Women painted in provocative poses, lounging in elegant beds or on chaise lounges, their bodies draped in silk or bare entirely. It was unheard of, scandalous, utterly bizarre in her little village, and now here was Erevos, her terrifying godlike companion, doing the very same thing without even realizing it.

After a good minute of laughter, Lyssena finally began to calm, her chest rising and falling with the soft aftershocks of joy, her smile lingering as she wiped away the tears that had gathered at the corners of her eyes.

She turned her gaze back to her god that was still reclined, still utterly motionless, still in that same absurd pose.

"It is very comfortable," Erevos said at last, voice low and matter-of-fact, and Lyssena mimicked him, leaning on one arm, bending her knee, and letting her foot dangle just as he had.

It was, she admitted to herself, indeed very comfortable. But when she adopted the pose, Erevos did not laugh.

He stared.

And though she couldn't fully explain the difference between *looking* and *staring* when it came to eyes like his, she had come to understand it all the same.

It was in the stillness, in the sharpness of his focus, in the way the air itself seemed to tighten around her when he observed her like this.

Erevos was not a man—nor a god—of many words, but he expressed so much with his eyes.

They were repressive things, devouring in their attention,

as if every time they landed on her, they peeled back another layer of her skin and soul.

Lyssena had also begun to notice that Erevos didn't have much body language at all.

When he stood, he stood straight. Never leaning, never slouching, never curling into himself like humans did.

He never blinked, never wrinkled the nose he did not have, never shifted weight from foot to foot.

He was always composed, always still, always caught in some divine stillness that made him seem carved from stone or shadow or both.

But now—here, in this new posture, and with that long, unwavering stare—Lyssena could feel something different pulsing just beneath the surface. Her Erevos felt warmer, not so distant. *Her* Erevos?

Erevos wasn't hers.

Certainly not.

How could a god belong to anyone? But then again . . . he had said he wasn't a god at all.

And she remembered his question from before—*What is a god, Lyssena?*

"A god is . . . " she began aloud, voice quiet, like she was answering a riddle. "Someone who can do anything. Someone who can grant wishes."

At that, Erevos reached for her hand, large and dark and warm, and pulled her gently toward him.

She glided without resistance, suddenly half on her back, half on her side, her body close enough to feel the radiant heat that pulsed from his chest, her eyes wide with surprise.

She didn't know why he had pulled her closer, but he was so big, and so warm, and so . . .

"What do you wish for?" he asked, his voice soft but impossibly deep, rumbling through her like distant thunder.

And now it was Lyssena who stared.

She stared into the endless purple of his gaze, stared at the way his mouth moved just slightly when he spoke, the barely-there twitch of motion that made him seem almost human.

"I wish for . . . " she exhaled, the breath catching slightly on its way out.

She didn't know what to say. Did she wish for him to kiss her?

The thought was absurd, and yet, why was it the first one that came to mind?

Erevos was a deeply masculine presence, too masculine for his own good, with his towering frame and low voice and the way he moved so gently despite the sheer force of him, and Lyssena found herself growing more and more confused.

He had seen her bare and had not reacted at all. Not a glance, not a shift, nothing.

And still, despite that indifference, despite that restraint, she kept thinking about it.

Even in this strange, godless place.

Chapter Twenty

The Pink of Spring

Erevos

His songbird smelled sweet again.

Erevos knew what sweetness was; he had tasted the purest form of devotion from Lyssena, warm and radiant like golden nectar on his tongue, but this scent was different.

It was still sweet, but in another way. Perhaps a different flavor entirely.

He watched her in silence, waiting as she thought through his question, and he knew, without a doubt, that whatever she wished for, he would give her all of it.

If she wanted more dresses, he would shape them from shadow and silk, would craft her every design her imagination could conjure.

If she desired more spices, he would find a dozen more Rolams, scour the corners of the human realm, and bring back every box and jar, every powder and seed that could make her food sing.

He would go back to the human world, again and again, if it meant placing a smile on her lips.

But more than anything, Erevos wished that Lyssena would never want to leave him.

Because if she did, he would not be able to let her go. He simply couldn't.

His little songbird was too precious, too lovely, too kind, too beautifully human to belong anywhere but here . . . wrapped in his arms, safe and kept, where he could protect her and hold her and never again let her be hurt.

And right now, with her lying so near, he felt that familiar desire to pull her close, to feel the weight of her body against his, to breathe in the sweet scent now radiating from her skin.

"What is it that you wish for?" he asked again as he lifted the arm he had been resting on and brought it above her, caging her beneath him.

"Tell me, Lyssena," he whispered, his face close to hers, his breath a caress of warmth. "What is it that you want?"

Her sweet scent deepened, and Erevos lowered his head to hers, his mouth barely an inch from her temple, and inhaled deeply.

Lyssena's lips twitched, as if she were about to say something but lost the thought at the very edge of her tongue.

Erevos knew she hadn't truly forgotten, so perhaps she had changed her mind; perhaps she was shifting through all the possibilities, weighing want against need, sorting the tangled threads of want and caution like he often did himself.

"I wish for you to answer two of my questions," she whispered at last, and Erevos went still.

He had been certain she would ask for an object—perhaps silk, or sugar, or another soft comfort—or ask him to do something for her, to build her something, or bring her something, or promise her something with his power.

But his songbird wanted answers.

And he would give her those, too.

"I promise not to joke this time," he said, his mouth stretching into that impossibly wide grin.

At that, Lyssena giggled. A sound light and fluttering, like the brush of wings across a mirror's surface, and it made his gaze drift over her face, tracing every shifting muscle, every twitch of her lips, the way her nose scrunched just slightly, the way her eyes shone with thought.

"Are you a man?"

A man meant a human male.

Erevos knew the term well enough. His body was shaped in a similar fashion, two arms, two legs, a head, a mouth, all the familiar signs of humanoid form, but that was where the similarity ended.

"I am not a human, Lyssena," he answered.

"I know that!" she said with a soft smile, and Erevos noticed that her green eyes were slowly being swallowed by the black dots in their centers.

"Are there gods that are wome—female?" she asked next, tilting her head on the pillow.

"I am no god," Erevos replied, "and there are no females of my kind."

Demons did not reproduce; there was no cycle, no mating, no need for such things in The Void. Erevos had never cared to question it, had never felt the need to, until Lyssena's soft, curious voice drew the thought from him.

He paused.

That demon he had erased . . .

He remembered it now. The grotesque mimicry, the blood, the stroking. He had seen human males rub themselves in the same manner, though only now did he understand the significance, the perversion of what had been done.

That demon had likely fed too deeply on lust, had drowned in it until it twisted him.

"So you're a male!" Lyssena said, her voice hesitant, the words curling upward into a question. "Uh . . . right?"

Was he?

Erevos glanced down at his body, at the legs that mirrored a man's well enough, the shape that had always simply *been*. He had legs, yes.

So . . . there was that.

As he turned his gaze back to Lyssena, he noticed that her face had changed color. Her cheeks and the tip of her nose now flushed a warm shade of pink, the exact hue of those soft-petaled flowers that bloomed in the human realm when spring began to stretch its fingers across the land.

The Void had no seasons.

It knew no cold or warmth, no change of light or wind, no changing of sky or soil. And yet Erevos had always been curious about how the world moved through its cycles, how color faded and returned, how trees shed and regrew, how snow, which he had only seen in the human realm, fell like frozen ash from the clouds.

But spring . . .

Spring was when the human realm became its most colorful, its most alive, and he remembered it vividly. It was in the spring that he'd seen Lyssena in one of the most memorable moments in his life.

She had been sitting beneath the angled bend of a tree whose trunk curved like a question, her form framed by a halo of pink blossoms that trembled in the wind, and she had looked ethereal.

The same shade dusted her cheeks now.

Songbirds sang the loudest when the world was pink and full of bloom, when the air was warm, and the sky was blue, and Erevos thought it suited her. His songbird, so full of color and warmth.

And in that moment, he thought he wanted to devour her, to cage her inside himself, to hold her so close she would never again be beyond reach, to fold her into his being until no part of her could be taken or lost.

Everything about her was just . . .

Perfect.

"Then I am a male, Lyssena. I can call myself god if you wish me to."

Chapter Twenty-One

Where Sweetness Lingered

Lyssena

Lyssena was so wet she didn't know what to do.

Erevos was too much all at once. Too overwhelming, too close, too intense, and she had no experience in situations like this.

She couldn't tell whether he was flirting with her or not, or if this was simply how Erevos always was—deep-voiced and calm, but with a way of speaking that melted her from the inside out.

She was lost.

All she could see was his face, his broad shoulders, the thick curve of his arms braced above her, his body a hovering menace she didn't fear but felt drowning in.

She breathed slowly, tried to keep herself calm, tried not to stare, but failed. Because how could she not look at him? Her male-non-god-god, as strange and beautiful as he was, and she found herself wanting . . . more.

She just didn't know *what* more meant yet.

Although . . . there was one thing.

She could *accidentally* lift her knee—just slightly—and finally discover whether there was *anything* there. She'd seen him standing, of course, had tried to look without staring, but whenever Erevos was facing her, he was always looking at her, and she had no idea what she was even looking for.

Before she could ask the second question that lingered in her mind, her knee lifted—just slightly, accidentally—and pressed against him.

And Erevos tensed.

She saw the way the muscles across his arms, shoulders, and neck tightened all at once, like cords pulled taut beneath his skin.

"Oh, I'm so sorry!" she blurted, her hands lifting instinctively, moving to his face without thinking, her palms cupping the sharp lines of his jaw.

She realized what she was doing only after the warmth of him burned against her skin, and she started to pull away—

But Erevos leaned down and caught her hands with his face again.

A low, deep sound rumbled from his chest, so heavy and deep that for a second, Lyssena thought the bed beneath them was about to crack apart.

As he lowered himself even closer, his body now brushing hers fully, she felt something hard pressing against her knee. Something very, very hard.

And growing.

"Why do you smell so sweet?" he murmured, his voice brushing against her nose. "Too sweet, songbird. What is that?"

Lyssena had been brave yesterday—and apparently, today as well—because the next thing that came out of her mouth was something scandalous, something she never imagined she would dare say aloud, or frankly, even think of.

With her heart pounding against her ribs, she whispered, "Could you find where it's coming from?"

And the moment the words left her lips, her hands flew up to her face, covering her cheeks in hot, trembling panic.

Since when did she speak like that?

Perhaps since her Erevos had reclined in that ridiculous, charming pose, or since his deep voice had started saying things that curled around her thoughts.

She wasn't entirely sure what he smelled on her, but she had a very specific suspicion. Maybe it was something wet. Something between her thighs.

At least . . . that was what she *secretly* wanted to believe, for no reason at all.

Right?

Erevos was so close now, so unbearably close, that if he had a nose, he would've surely bumped it against her hands from how quickly and firmly she pressed them against her burning face.

After a long, low hum, he dipped his head to the crook of her neck and inhaled again, and Lyssena exhaled just as deeply, unable to hold it in, her breath trembling on the way out.

No man had ever looked at her like Erevos did—unblinking, intense, as though her soul lived beneath her skin and he could see it—and after asking a question so sinful, so suggestive, having him stare into her eyes now was challenging to think of anything.

She could barely hold it.

The room was so quiet that all Lyssena could hear—besides the frantic thrum of her own heartbeat—was the shifting of sheets as Erevos moved lower, his massive body sliding down the bed as he sought the source of the sweet scent he had spoken of.

He passed over her breasts, though Lyssena found herself

wishing he might linger there for just a moment. But he didn't stop.

And when he reached just above her belly button, a high-pitched, involuntary sound slipped from her throat—half gasp, half whimper—and Erevos paused, lifting his gaze to hers.

"My apologies," he said, and lifted himself back up, rising to sit on his heels.

It was only then that Lyssena realized her eyes had been closed.

She had been so tense, so consumed by everything happening around and inside her, that she hadn't even noticed how her nerves had taken control.

She blinked, staring at the ceiling above her—a canopy of black and lace—and tried to breathe, tried to anchor herself in something real before turning her eyes toward Erevos.

And what she saw made her breath catch all over again.

There were spikes—thick, long, jagged spikes—jutting from the back of his head, down along his spine in a sharp, dangerous trail that hadn't been there before.

They were a continuation of him, a part of him, as if they were always there.

They hadn't been there before. She was sure of it.

Was this normal for him? Was it a sickness? Could gods . . . get sick?

And if Erevos truly *wasn't* a god, as he claimed—and she still didn't entirely believe that—could whatever he was grow spikes like this? Did his kind change shape when touched, when aroused, when . . . affected?

"I have scared you," Erevos said, his hands resting calmly on his thighs, his voice heavy. "I should have asked if I could be so close to you."

Lyssena slowly lifted herself onto her elbows, then into a sitting position, her wide eyes locked onto him.

She shook her head as if trying to wake from a dream—but this wasn't a dream.

It couldn't be possible for her to be lying here beside someone so powerful.

It couldn't be possible that she had spoken the way she had, so boldly, so shamelessly.

And it was *absolutely* impossible for her god—her Erevos—to change his form right before her eyes.

"You have spikes . . . " she murmured, her gaze moving slowly between each and every thorn that had grown from his body.

"Spikes?" Erevos asked, and he truly looked as surprised as she was.

Chapter Twenty-Two

What Hunger Shapes

Erevos

It was difficult to concentrate with such sweetness lingering in the air, but Erevos had to.

He rose from the bed and rolled his shoulders slowly, feeling his muscles beneath skin that no longer felt entirely his. Now that he was standing, the weight of the new spikes along his spine and head felt like a string of thorns that had grown from within.

"I know what it is," he said to his songbird, who was still watching him with parted lips and wide eyes that flicked up and down his body. Her gaze lingered downward—longer than it lingered upward—and Erevos followed it, expecting to find another change.

And he did.

It wasn't like the spikes on his back or the ones that fanned out from his head, which he could now feel when he lifted a hand to trace them. No, this one was . . . different, not so "spiky" at the tip.

"The spikes on my back are not like this one between my legs," he said.

He considered how best to explain the nature of demonkind, how bodies changed with emotion, and how The Void shaped its children according to what they fed on. It was not something Erevos had ever needed to explain. It was simply known.

"This wasn't supposed to happen," he said at last. "Not to me." He glided his hand over one of the spikes.

"When a demon consumes too much of a particular emotion, it takes a toll on its body. Sometimes the change is visible. Sometimes it lies dormant, hidden deep beneath the skin until it awakens."

Lyssena blinked, her lashes brushing the tops of her cheeks, and Erevos took it as a sign to continue.

"I've consumed rage before," he said, lowering himself onto the bed beside her, the mattress shifting beneath his weight. "But never enough to feel it etched onto my body. Not until now." He paused, then added, "Yesterday . . . I did. And now rage has left its mark on me."

"Does it hurt?" she asked, her voice small, brows knitting.

Erevos felt warmth in his chest, not fire, but something gentler. Something soft. Lyssena still smelled sweet, but it was no longer the same sweetness from before. It had changed. And Erevos, for all his knowing, could not yet decipher it.

"It doesn't hurt," he said, dropping his gaze to his hands.

What was this? This warmth inside him—so constant now, so strangely good—what did it mean? He had been warm ever since Lyssena entered his world, warm in ways that had nothing to do with the nature of his body. Had she given him emotions? Shown him how they felt?

Erevos wanted to understand it.

But more than that, he wanted her to understand it, too.

"I've killed the demon who frightened you," he said finally. "I've erased him from The Void."

Lyssena said nothing for a while. She simply looked at him, her hands curled into the sheets at her sides. Erevos could feel her breath brushing the air between them.

"You said demons change from emotions," she said quietly, and Erevos dipped his chin.

"It happens," he replied. "When a demon feeds too deeply from a single emotion, his body . . . begins to reflect it."

He had seen that happen with many of his kind. Not all, but too many to count.

"Spikes are the mark of rage. But not all demons crave such things."

"What other emotions can do that?" Lyssena asked.

"Sorrow can change the body. Some demons lose their shape, their skin constantly dripping like weeping shadows. Others become smoke, formless, unable to hold onto anything because they have consumed too much despair."

He paused, then added, "There are those who favor trust. They appear soft, hollowed, their backs open and defenseless."

Lyssena's eyes grew wide again. "And that?" she asked, lifting one hand to point down toward the new hardness straining between his legs.

For a moment, Erevos said nothing.

Then his eyes dropped to where she pointed. "That," he said, "is not from rage."

He moved a hand toward himself, trailing it down his abdomen, until it brushed the hardness she'd indicated.

And at the moment of contact, heat bloomed like the briefest caress of her knee from before.

"It feels the same as when you touched me," he said, gaze returning to hers. "When your knee brushed it. That's when it began."

Lyssena was still.

Erevos flexed his hand and hovered above the new organ. "Can I touch it?" he asked. He wanted to feel this heat again. He did not know what it was, but it felt very good. So good, he even wanted his songbird to try.

"You *do* have a cock . . . " Lyssena breathed, and Erevos turned his gaze fully toward her, drawn by the sound of her voice as much as the words themselves. She was half-sitting on the bed now, her arms braced in front of her as they held her weight, her body angled toward him as she leaned closer.

A cock, Erevos thought. A male genitalia.

"I never had one before," he said slowly, as if speaking the words aloud might help them settle into sense.

He tried to understand why his body had changed this way, why this particular shape had formed between his legs when it never had before. That other demon had possessed one—the one he had erased—and perhaps this, too, was the result of excess, of feeding too long and too deeply on lust until the body bent itself to accommodate it.

Erevos had never consumed lust. He simply had never sought it.

Or . . . had he?

His gaze returned to Lyssena. To the way her green-apple eyes were fixed on him without flinching. To the way her lips were parted, and how her arms pressed inward, squeezing the mounds of her chest together as she leaned forward.

They looked fuller now than before, heavier somehow. *They might be as soft as her cheeks,* he thought that, too.

The first time Lyssena had touched his shadows, he had felt that warmth bloom inside him, and it had returned again and again since then, growing stronger each time she drew closer, until now, with his songbird nearer to him than she had ever been, he felt himself teetering at the edge of something he could not name, something that threatened to unmake him entirely.

Could that be attraction?

Erevos did not know. But he wanted to.

He lifted his hand again and wrapped his fingers around the new length between his thighs, circling it experimentally, and his hips jerked forward at once as though his body had acted entirely on its own.

What was this sensation?

If Erevos's eyes were capable of widening, they would have done so now.

"Lyssena," he breathed, startled enough by the sudden surge of pleasure that he pulled his hand away as quickly as he had touched himself, the heat lingering even after contact was broken.

His songbird had changed color.

She no longer merely had the eyes of a green apple. Now her face had taken on the deep, flushed red of one as well, her cheeks and nose burning bright as one hand flew up to cover her mouth, her body going utterly still.

Erevos studied her reaction carefully. Was this a human gesture? Had Lyssena covered her mouth so he would not put his new cock inside it?

Oh. If the simple pressure of his hand had felt like *that*—if it had drawn such a response from his body so quickly—then what would her lips feel like, soft and warm, closing around him instead?

His gaze dropped back down to himself, to the rigid length standing proud and unyielding between his legs, hard as his head, pulsing with life and heat.

"I don't know much about it," Lyssena said, though her voice came out smaller than before, softened and partially swallowed behind her palm, and as she slowly lowered her hand, the tip of her finger caught on her lower lip, tugging it down just a little before it went up again.

That single, absent gesture claimed Erevos's attention completely.

For a long moment, he could not hold onto her words at all, could not remember what she had said or why, because his thoughts had narrowed to the curve of her mouth, the slight press of her fingertip against her lip, and the sudden, unfamiliar awareness of his own body responding to the smallest movement of hers.

And then she crawled closer.

Her knees brushed against his left thigh as she moved, the contact light, yet it sent a pulse through him, as though her touch had traced a hidden seam beneath his skin and set something loose inside him.

"Before my engagement," Lyssena continued, "my mother taught me how to please a man."

The word *engagement* struck Erevos.

That human male—the one who had dared to believe she might belong to him, the one who had frightened her, *wanted* her—rose in his mind in a flash of cold, and for a moment, Erevos felt the familiar, corrosive pull of rage coil tight in his chest, sharp enough that the spikes along his spine twitched in response, ready to bloom again.

"I hope you don't mind," Lyssena murmured.

Her hand settled on his thigh first, and then her other hand closed around him.

Erevos's thoughts vanished.

Her grip was gentle, her fingers sliding along his length in slow motions that sent sensation spiraling through him in waves, every pass of her hand leaving behind heat and pressure and something dangerously close to ache, so overwhelming in its novelty that his muscles flexed on their own.

"Lyssena—" he groaned, the sound torn from him before he could shape it, before he could stop it.

He had never felt anything like this in all of his existence.

The only comparison his mind could grasp was the moment she had tasted the bread he had made for her, the way something warm and unsteady had bloomed inside him then, too, as though her pleasure had reached into him and changed him from within.

He watched her hand move, transfixed by the way her fingers circled him, by the contrast between her soft skin and the rigid heat of his body. He lifted his gaze to her face and found her watching him just as closely, her eyes framed by her lashes.

Her scent returned all at once.

It flooded the air between them, thick and sweet and intoxicating, far stronger than before, curling around him until it felt as though it had weight, as though he could sink into it and be lost entirely, and Erevos realized that he wanted exactly that. He wanted to drown in her sweetness, in her hands, in whatever this new, uncharted thing between them was becoming.

Lyssena's breathing slowed, each inhale deeper than the last, and Erevos could hear the quiet pull of oxygen into her fragile, human lungs, the soft release as she let it out again. And the awareness of it filled him with a fondness he did not yet know how to name.

He adored that.

He adored that his songbird breathed the air he shaped for her, that her chest rose and fell because he allowed the atmosphere of his realm to cradle her, that she wore garments spun from his shadows against her skin, that her hands held his cock without fear, without hesitation, and that she no longer looked at him as something to flee from.

Erevos adored Lyssena.

With her fingers still wrapped around him and that thick, intoxicating sweetness pouring from her in waves, he leaned his torso toward her, drawn by instinct alone, and slid his right arm around her waist, pulling her closer until their bodies met fully, and the sudden shift in balance sent them both tumbling onto the soft bed beneath them.

Lyssena gasped in surprise.

The sound vibrated through him, and her hand tightened reflexively around his cock, squeezing just as Erevos lost whatever fragile restraint he had left and collapsed over her, his weight braced carefully so as not to crush her, though every part of him burned with heat and pressure and the overwhelming need to be closer still.

The sensation crested too quickly.

His body seized, arching into hers as something dark and warm spilled from him in thick pulses, smeared across her new dress, staining her with him, and Erevos groaned low in his chest as the force of it tore through him, leaving him trembling and utterly undone atop his songbird.

Chapter Twenty-Three

The Shape of a God

Lyssena

On one hand, Erevos had killed another god and Kaan.

On the other, he had saved her—twice.

Lyssena knew death well. She had seen it often enough throughout her life that, at some point, there was no longer a place for tears to go, no reason left to cry when the inevitable came to pass. She did not wish death upon herself, ever, but when it came for someone she did not know, it troubled her less than she believed it should.

In her village, executions were common enough to become part of the rhythm of life, spoken of in low, solemn tones and accepted without question. People could be beheaded for so many reasons— for infidelity, when a wife failed to commit herself properly to her husband; for looking a man in the eyes without permission; for avoiding marriage without a justifica-tion deemed acceptable, such as a calling to work with herbs; or for bearing too many children who were, for reasons no one ever explained, too beautiful to be trusted.

There were so many reasons women were killed.

Women.

How was it that Lyssena had never noticed before—truly noticed— that it was only women who were punished this way? How was it that no man was ever burned at the stake for being unfaithful, no husband ever dragged into the square and judged for wandering hands or broken vows?

The realization settled slowly, quietly, like dust finally visible in a beam of light.

Lyssena understood then that it was not something she had been blind to by accident, but something she had never thought to question, because it had always been this way. It was normal. It was expected. It was woven so deeply into the fabric of her world that she had accepted it without ever wondering why.

She had realized so much since coming to this place, so much since meeting her god.

The thought made her smile.

How could Erevos insist that he was not a god when every-thing about him suggested otherwise? He was a creator—and a clever one at that—compassionate, merciful, powerful, and protective in all the ways she had been taught a god should be. Erevos was everything she believed a god to be, and she could not understand why he denied it so firmly, why he chose to call himself a demon instead.

Perhaps that was simply what gods called themselves.

There had been stories, once, whispered warnings that demons hunted the sinful, dragged them away into darkness to be punished for their transgressions. Lyssena had never paid them much mind before, but now the thought returned to her, curious rather than frightening.

Was she sinful?

She had stroked her god's cock, after all. And she was not even married to him.

Perhaps that was her first sin.

Maybe the second. She was, after all, a woman.

After lying in bed with Erevos, her skin still coated in his dark semen, he led Lyssena to wash, guiding her to the hot spring bathing room before leaving her there alone so he could finish crafting her oxygen mask.

The cave-like chamber, carved from stone and shadow, was warm and damp against her skin. The last time she had stood here—yesterday, she assumed—Erevos had washed her himself, using a bar of shadowy soap that smelled of almost nothing at all, save for the faintest trace of cinnamon, one of the spices he kept inside that eggshell-colored box full of strange, wonderful things from her world.

She found the soap exactly where they had left it, resting on one of the smooth rocks beside the inky, steaming water, and her gaze drifted briefly to the entrance as she wondered whether her white gown and undergarments were waiting for her in the new closet he had made for her, freshly cleaned by hands that could shape shadows but also, apparently, care for such small, human necessities.

Lyssena had always been a curious person.

As she stepped closer to the water, she found herself wondering whether her god had ever needed to clean this place at all, whether dust could exist in The Void, whether time left residue here the way it did in the human world, gathering quietly in corners when no one was looking.

But those questions would have to wait.

Since arriving in this strange new home, she had not relieved herself even once—not since the moment Erevos had taken her from her world—and the pressure had grown steadily more noticeable.

Erevos had explained to her that he had created a system in which her waste would break down into particles and be carried forward through time itself, scattered into space, because he understood how atoms worked, how time moved and bent and folded in ways humans could not yet comprehend.

Of course, Lyssena understood none of that.

"Humans didn't get to it yet," she murmured aloud, repeating his words with a smile as her voice echoed around the chamber, "and probably never will."

When Lyssena finished bathing, her thoughts settled stubbornly on two things, circling them again and again as though unable to decide which deserved her attention more.

The first was her Erevos's dark semen. She knew, at least in theory, what it was meant to look like, as her mother had spent the past few months instructing her, speaking in hushed, serious tones about a husband's body and the signs of his pleasure. And yet none of those lessons had prepared her for how strange and intimate it had felt to be coated in it.

The second was the oxygen mask.

Not just that Erevos was making one for her, but that he was shaping it like a songbird.

Her god could make her bodily waste disappear into nothingness, could bend matter and time in ways she could barely begin to imagine, could create air itself so that her fragile lungs might continue to draw breath, and the thought settled heavily in her chest as understanding slowly took shape.

Lyssena realized, perhaps for the first time, how deeply dependent she truly was.

How easily Erevos could take her life if he wished.

The knowledge did not arrive as fear so much as clarity, and as she stepped out of the bathing chamber, she noticed that the once-terrifying hallway beyond was now lit by the same gray orbs she had seen in her rooms.

It was not as frightening as it had been before, but it was still . . . unsettling.

She knew the demon-god who had called to her earlier was gone now. She had proof of that etched directly into Erevos's body, in the dangerous spikes that marked what he had done to protect her.

Still, walking alone through a dark corridor lit only by a handful of floating lights felt strange, too quiet, too hollow.

So Lyssena did what she had always done when the world felt uncertain.

She hummed a simple tune beneath her breath and kept walking.

To her left, Lyssena noticed that the space widened. The narrow passage opened into a broader stretch of shadow stone where the walls curved outward, forming what looked like the perfect place for a living room. At its center stood a door.

Not the kind of door she had ever seen in a home, but one that was heavy, tall, and looked like the great double doors of the temple. To be exact, it looked *identical* to them, from the angular shape of the wood to the familiar curve of the handles.

"You saw the door."

Erevos's voice echoed through the corridor, and Lyssena's heart began to beat faster, each thud loud in her ears as she turned toward the sound.

He stood at the far end of the hallway, partially framed by shadow, holding the face of a songbird. Her oxygen mask.

"Yes," she said quietly, unable to stop herself from staring at him.

In the dim light, Erevos's eyes glowed a deep purple, like twin stars falling through a darkened sky, and when his mouth curved upward in response, he revealed every row and set of his sharp teeth in a smile that was far too wide to be anything but his.

Chapter Twenty-Four

Between Breath and Death

Lyssena

Lyssena waited for Erevos to cross the hallway.

Was she finally going to see what this strange, new world looked like?

She wondered whether everything beyond those doors was made of shadows, just like the home Erevos had carved. She wanted to know what kind of flowers grew here, whether their petals would feel cool or warm beneath her fingertips, whether they carried scent at all, or if even fragrance dissolved into something thinner in this place. She wanted to know what stories the view would tell her, whether the horizon would stretch endlessly and black or shimmer with colors her human eyes had never been meant to witness.

She wanted to know where the gods lived.

Lyssena felt slightly uneasy at the way Erevos did not blink as he walked toward her with a full grin, the head of a songbird cradled in his hands. He stopped half a step before her and stretched his hand forward.

"For you," he said, offering the mask that would allow her to breathe.

How, she did not know.

Lyssena took it carefully, her fingers brushing against feathers that were not truly feathers at all but beautiful ridges shaped from shadow. She noticed every stitch along the edges, each thread woven from darkness. The mask barely weighed anything in her palms, light as a whisper, and yet it was entirely sealed, without a single visible opening through which air might pass.

"What would happen if I tried to breathe without it?" she asked, shifting her gift slowly from side to side between her hands, watching the gray light catch along the curve of the beak.

"You will die."

At that, Lyssena stilled, the beak caught between her fingers as though it might snap if she held it too tightly. "I understand. Thank you," she said, and Erevos did not move.

She had noticed that since she had stroked his cock, Erevos lingered when he looked at her, his gaze heavier, as though something had changed between them that neither of them had yet named. It had not happened long ago, she was certain of that, for she had never bathed for too long in her home, otherwise her brothers would scold her and remind her she was no princess to soak in lavish waters while others worked.

Well.

Now she was a shadow princess, with a crown resting on the drawer beside her velvety bed.

Her brothers could not—and would absolutely not—scold her now. She could do whatever she pleased, linger as long as she wished, breathe strange air through a bird-shaped mask, because her god was kind, merciful, and frighteningly capable of reshaping the world itself for her.

With those thoughts settling in her head, she turned toward the doors and wrapped her fingers around the handle.

It took her several seconds to realize that Erevos's face was right in front of hers.

So close that she could see the glow of purple in his eyes shift and deepen. So close that the faint scent of cinnamon and shadow surrounded her again. So close that if she leaned forward even the smallest fraction, her lips would brush against sharp teeth that were not made for gentle things.

"You need to put the mask on first."

Right.

Lyssena had been so eager to see the world beyond those heavy doors that she had nearly stepped forward and into her own death if her god had not stopped her in time.

She noticed then the way Erevos was standing, hunched so that his glowing eyes met hers at the same level, and yet most of his body was not entirely inside the house at all.

It was inside the door.

Not pressed against it.

Not blocked by it.

Inside it.

Shadow seemed to ripple where his torso disappeared into the dark wood, as though the material welcomed him, as though the boundary between object and body did not exist for him the way it did for her.

Could he simply walk through shadowed walls and closed doors as though they were mist?

Lyssena found herself wondering whether this house was not merely something Erevos had created, but something that was, in some incomprehensible way, part of him. An extension of his will. A body larger than the one that stood before her.

The thought sent a small shiver down her spine.

She had to remind herself that the rules she had grown up

with—the rules of wood and iron and flesh and consequence—did not apply here. They had no authority in this strange realm where time folded and air was crafted by hand and death waited patiently on the other side of a door.

So Lyssena made a decision.

Later, when they returned from whatever waited for her beyond these doors, she would give herself a small mission.

She would explore and observe.

She would learn how this place worked, how the shadows breathed, how the walls listened, how far her god's presence truly stretched.

Erevos stood in silence, waiting for Lyssena to put on her mask.

She lifted it slightly, turning it this way and that in her hands as she searched for some visible fastening, some ribbon or clasp that would tell her how a human was meant to wear such a thing—but she found nothing.

"I don't know how to wear it, Greatest," she admitted.

"You bent my shadows yesterday."

She had.

She had shaped animals from shadows, formed weapons with trembling fingers, and finally crafted a crown worthy of resting upon her own head. So she nodded at the hint her god had given her and steadied her breath, allowing the memory of that strange sensation—the yielding, living quality of shadow—to return to her fingertips.

"Would you help me put it on?" she asked. "I would like to wear you."

The moment those words left Lyssena's lips, the back of the mask unfurled.

It did not snap or hinge open like metal or leather, but rather ... softened.

The shadow along its spine loosened and parted as though

it had been waiting for permission, revealing a hollow interior that seemed deeper than it should have been.

Lyssena inhaled sharply and lifted it toward her face.

It was a strange experience, witnessing something inanimate respond to her voice, to her wish, watching an unmoving thing come alive.

As the beak aligned with her nose and mouth, she felt a long chill crawl up her spine and settle at the base of her neck, like cold fingers tracing along her skin. The mask sealed itself around her head without pressure or force, closing in a seamless line that vanished the moment it met her temples.

Lyssena felt nothing. It was neither cool nor warm, neither heavy nor light.

It was like Erevos.

And before she could turn her head from side to side to test how well it adjusted to her movements, she felt more of that same nothingness spilling downward, flowing over her shoulders and along her arms in a tide.

Her gown responded. The fabric her god had created for her darkened and extended, lengthening to the tips of her fingers, curling around her wrists, sliding down over her hips and thighs, stretching to her heels and toes as though shadow itself were blooming from the seams. Lyssena stood utterly still as it finished.

She was covered in shadows.

And yet it felt as though she was covered in nothing at all. No weight, no friction, no fabric brushing against her skin, only the faintest awareness that she had been claimed by something that fit her too perfectly to be separate from her.

Lyssena bent her knees slowly, testing the balance of her new form, then stretched her arms as high above her head as she could. She shook her head from side to side, the beak of the mask remaining perfectly aligned with her breath, and wiggled her torso.

Her full shadow bodysuit fit flawlessly.

It did not tug or wrinkle. It did not resist her at all.

To anyone else, the display might have looked silly—a grown woman swaying and stretching as though she had just discovered her limbs—but Lyssena noticed that she began testing the edges of her comfort, to push against the boundaries of what she was given and see how her god would respond.

She liked to see whether he would correct her, restrain her, or even punish her.

So far, he had not minded at all.

Not when she spoke too boldly. Not when she questioned him. Not even when she had wrapped her hand around his cock and stroked him without instruction.

And that absence of punishment had begun to unfurl something inside her.

It made her move more freely. It made her speak her thoughts more often, even if not always, even if sometimes she still caught herself before words escaped her tongue. But still more than she ever had before.

For the first time in her life, Lyssena felt special.

Not merely tolerated or useful. Special.

She felt like a splash of color in a world carved from shadow. She had no village laws pressing against her ribs, no watchful eyes measuring the length of her bath or the sharpness of her tongue, and even if freedom required an oxygen mask shaped like a bird's face, she would wear it gladly if it meant she could walk where she pleased and lift her chin without fear.

And now, she was going to see what lay beyond those doors.

She was going to see The Void.

The thought sent a bright thrill through her chest, and she could not stop the small, excited breath that escaped her beneath the beak.

Chapter Twenty-Five

Shadow and Air

Erevos

When his songbird finished moving in place, Erevos finally allowed himself to take a proper look at his newest creation.

His darkness had swallowed her whole, sealing itself along every curve and hollow, and the sight pleased him more than he thought it would.

Lyssena was breathing the air he provided from the human realm, air stolen and folded through time and space. It was not the first time she had done so; she had breathed it within their home, beneath his ceilings, within walls that answered to him. She still did. But now she carried it with her.

What excited him, what stirred something sharp and hungry beneath his skin, was not merely that she could breathe, but that he could manipulate that fragile oxygen across realms and distances, thread it through shadow and eternity, and let his songbird carry it wherever she wished to wander.

Since she had asked him whether she was still inside a cage, the question unsettled him. Erevos had resolved that she would never feel that way again.

For his greatest wish—his most consuming desire—was to make her stay.

Forever.

He had given her a home shaped from himself. He had arranged meals suitable for human flesh. He had drawn baths that held her gently instead of devouring her. And now he knew she could breathe without dying in his realm.

He had tested the mask on a deer first.

The creature had trembled as he fitted the shadowed beak over its snout, its pulse frantic beneath thin skin, its dark eyes wide with a terror that meant nothing to him—not when compared to the thought of risking Lyssena's life. He had watched the animal step beyond the threshold, had watched it live.

Only then had he allowed himself to place such a thing in her hands.

Now it was finally time for his songbird to see the outside.

With those thoughts, Erevos opened both doors. He kept his gaze fixed on hers as the shadows parted, watching her masked eyes, watching the subtle lift of her shoulders as anticipation threaded through her body. He had believed he was eager to show her The Void, just as he had been eager to feed her, to bathe her, to clothe her, to provide, to shape, to give.

But as he stood there, shadow curling around his wrists, he realized that his eagerness was not about The Void at all.

It was about her reaction to it.

He wanted to see awe flood her.

He wanted to see fear flicker and then soften.

He wanted to know whether she would step forward on her own.

He would feed her. Bathe her. Clothe her. Build worlds beneath her feet if she desired them.

He would do everything. Anything.

As long as she chose to remain at his side.

Erevos stepped aside, the shadows parting with him, allowing Lyssena to take her first step beyond the threshold of their home.

"You can breathe, Lyssena," he said when he realized he could not hear the soft rhythm of her inhaling; her chest did not rise, did not fall. "Open your eyes."

He wanted to see the muted green of them through the thin sockets of the mask, wanted proof that she was truly looking, truly standing in a place no human had ever been meant to stand.

"I'm scared," she murmured, her voice small beneath the beak.

Then she gasped. "I can breathe!"

Of course, she could.

Erevos's mouth stretched wide in satisfaction, revealing rows of sharp, immaculate teeth. He was a clever demon, a demon who could bend matter, fold time, steal oxygen from another realm, and make it obey.

As his songbird took another step, and then another, moving farther from the doorway, turning in place as though testing whether the world would remain stable beneath her feet, gasping again and again simply because she could, Erevos did not follow.

He stood where he was and watched.

He found himself wondering whether the absence of color would disturb her eventually. Whether a human eye, raised in brightness and bloom, might find his realm lacking. To him, it was complete. It was vast and endless in ways that did not require decoration.

But humans were fragile things. They often mistook simplicity for emptiness.

Still, she had not complained. Not about the shadows or the darkness. Not about the way his home had been carved from a palette that belonged only to him.

And that pleased him.

Lyssena turned back toward him then, her movements quick, her eyes wide behind the mask. "I can't believe this place is even real."

Erevos tilted his head slightly at that, the shadows at his shoulders shifting with the motion.

"It is real. It is The Void," he said, and the only thing he could look upon was his shadow-songbird with wide, green eyes.

Chapter Twenty-Six

Beyond the Mouth of Stone

Lyssena

Lyssena had expected stepping outside to feel like falling, like crossing some invisible edge where the world would drop away beneath her feet, but instead Erevos turned, and the world did not open; it narrowed.

He did not lead her immediately into vastness, but deeper into stone.

The doorway did not spill into the sky, but into a cavern so immense she could not see its ceiling, only the suggestion of curvature where shadow thickened and swallowed detail whole. Her steps echoed very faintly against rock that seemed to drink sound rather than return it, and when she glanced back, the house was already smaller than it should have been, as though distance behaved differently here.

"You built this house inside a cave," she said, her voice soft, and yet it seemed to travel farther than it should. Lyssena thought of what would happen if she screamed.

Erevos did not answer immediately. He simply walked.

And so she followed.

The stone beneath her feet was not rough like the quarry walls near her village; it was smoother, it looked polished in places, as though countless unseen hands had brushed against it over centuries, though she suspected nothing had touched it at all. When she trailed her fingers along the cavern wall, the surface felt cool but not cold, solid but faintly yielding.

They turned once. Then again.

And again.

Lyssena began to lose her sense of direction, for the cavern did not twist in sharp angles but in slow, curving bends that made it impossible to measure distance. The walls narrowed and widened unpredictably, at times pressing closer as though curious about her, at others opening into vast hollows where the darkness pooled thickly between stone pillars that rose like the trunks of ancient trees.

"Do you know where we're going?" she asked, though she suspected the question was foolish.

Erevos glanced back at her, and even through the mask, she felt the weight of his amusement. Of course, he knew.

The cave floor shifted gradually beneath her covered feet, the stone giving way to a fine layer of dark sediment that gathered at the edges of her steps and then smoothed itself again. She slowed, crouching slightly, pressing her fingers into it.

It clung to her glove like ash.

But when she lifted her hand, it fell away without leaving residue. She straightened quickly, heart fluttering, both unsettled and delighted.

This cave was definitely not like the caves at her home.

The ceiling arched lower in one stretch, forcing Erevos to dip his head, though she suspected he did not need to, suspected he simply chose to.

They turned again.

Lyssena was certain now that if she tried to find her way back alone, she would wander endlessly until she forgot what she had been looking for.

"Are we close?" she asked, and only then did she notice that Erevos had stopped.

The cavern ahead brightened.

Not with light, but with absence of thickness, as though the darkness thinned into something translucent.

Erevos extended one hand behind him, not touching her, but close enough that she felt the suggestion of it. "Stay near me."

Lyssena nodded, and the final bend opened.

This was where the cave ended.

Lyssena stepped out of stone and into something that felt both infinite and unfinished.

The first thing she noticed was what she did not feel.

There was no wind.

Her bodysuit did not stir. The air did not rustle the feathers on her mask or slip around her ankles. It simply held in stillness so complete that her own small movements felt almost loud. So she took another step.

The grass beneath her was similar to what she knew, though the blades were darker than anything she had ever seen. When she bent and brushed her fingers through it, the texture was cool and silky, each strand thin and perfectly formed, bending easily and then rising again without resistance.

It did not smell like grass.

It did not smell like anything.

It was unusual . . . not to smell a single thing, something that Lyssena could not imagine getting used to. What would it be like if she lived here for years?

Though she did smell the food Erevos cooked for her.

Speaking of which . . . Lyssena turned to look at him. He was standing a few steps away from her, unmoving as usual.

He observed her, of that she was certain. He did so quite often, and she did not mind. Well, maybe she even enjoyed it a little more than a human should.

Lyssena decided it was not the time for lovey-dovey thoughts about her god, so she looked away, beyond the field stretched trees.

She walked toward the nearest one without asking permission.

Its trunk was the color of deep pomegranate, ridged and twisting upward into branches that spread wide but carried no fluttering leaves.

She pressed her palm against the bark, and that, too, felt like nothing.

"Are you alive?" she whispered, unsure whether she meant the tree or the realm itself.

It did not answer.

But she felt something faintly responsive beneath her touch, a subtle vibration that traveled from bark into bone. Lyssena stepped back, turning slowly.

There was no sky as she understood it.

Above her stretched an expanse of uninterrupted darkness, not clouded, not star-strewn, not lit by sun or moon, but vast and depthless, as though she stood inside the pupil of an eye. Her breath came quicker. The sheer scale of this place felt like she was trapped inside a dark dream.

To her left, she saw a current barely moving. A river, perhaps?

She had not noticed it at first, for it did not gleam or reflect in any familiar way. But as she moved farther from the cave's mouth, she saw a ribbon of black cutting through the land, smooth and very silent.

Lyssena decided to approach it. The water—if it was water —ran without ripple, without splash, without sound. When she crouched at its edge, she expected to see her reflection distorted along its surface. Instead, she saw nothing. Just depth.

She leaned closer, heart pounding.

"Erevos," she called, though she did not look away to meet her god's eyes.

The river did not mirror her mask, nor her hands, nor the outline of her form. It swallowed light entirely, leaving only an impression of endless descent.

Carefully, she extended one finger and dipped it into the surface.

The sensation was not wet.

It was cool and fluid, but it did not cling to her, did not bead or drip. When she lifted her finger, no trace remained, though she could swear the river had thickened briefly around her touch.

She stood abruptly, a thrill running through her. "This is impossible," she breathed.

The silence pressed around her ears until she became aware of her own heartbeat, steady and loud within her chest, the only rhythm in a place that did not seem to pulse at all. No insects hummed. No birds called. No leaves rustled. Even her footsteps felt swallowed the moment they landed.

She turned in a slow circle and thought to herself how this place felt like standing at the beginning of creation.

Or the end of it.

She looked back toward the cave mouth, where Erevos stood watching her, tall and unmoving near the threshold. For a fleeting moment, the enormity of the place made her feel small.

Lyssena lifted her chin, turning once more toward the endless stretch of dark grass and pomegranate-colored trees and silent rivers that refused to reflect her.

"I want to see all of it," she said.

And she meant it from the bottom of her heart.

When Lyssena was finally done with exploring every single tree within reach, every patch of ashy grass, every slow current of ink-dark water that refused to reflect her face, no matter how long she stared into it, she made her way back to Erevos, who had not moved from the place where she had left him.

Not once.

The entire time—though she could not say how much time had truly passed, for there was no sun to climb or sink, no moon to wax or wane, no shifting light to measure the hours—Erevos had remained exactly as he was. A figure carved from shadow itself.

He had watched her.

She knew that without needing to look.

Even when she wandered farther into the grass, even when she circled the trees and crouched by the riverbanks and pressed her palm against bark, she had felt the weight of his gaze resting between her shoulder blades. Only sometimes would his head turn slowly, following her path.

At first, it had unsettled her.

The awareness of being watched so intently, so continuously, had made her movements feel exaggerated. She had nearly stumbled once beneath the sensation, suddenly conscious of how small she must look against the endless dark.

And after a while, Lyssena found herself growing accustomed to it. Somehow.

It was like the silence of The Void. Overwhelming at first,

then gradually folding into the background of her awareness until it became part of the landscape itself.

When she finally reached him, she slowed her steps. Up close, he looked exactly as he had before she left—posture straight, shoulders relaxed, hands at his sides, darkness curling faintly around his form as though it breathed with him even when he did not visibly breathe. Had he truly not moved once?

"Did you just . . . stand here?" she asked, tilting her head slightly as she studied him.

If she had not known better, she might have believed him to be a statue erected in the mouth of the cave like some guardian figure carved to oversee the realm beyond.

Lyssena hesitated, her fingers fidgeting lightly at her sides. She wanted to ask him whether he was bored. The question hovered on her tongue.

On one hand, he was a god—or a demon—or something that blurred the boundary between the two so completely that the distinction hardly mattered. He shaped air and stone and shadow; he bent objects as though they were cloth. The concept of boredom might be too small and too human to apply to him at all.

But on the other hand, she could not help herself.

Curiosity rose in her, and she had begun to understand something about Erevos . . . something quite certain.

He did not get angry easily. In fact, he did not seem to get angry at all.

She had questioned him repeatedly. She had touched him boldly. She had stepped into his realm and asked whether she was caged. And he had never punished her.

The absence of wrath had made her braver.

"I was gone for . . . a while, I think," she said slowly, glancing back over the dark field as though it might offer some clue. "Were you bored?"

There it was. The word felt almost absurd in this place, where time did not pass the way it should.

She searched his face carefully for any flicker of offense, any tightening of shadow.

None came.

In truth, she had begun to suspect something that made warmth coil unexpectedly in her chest. She thought Erevos might enjoy her questions.

The way his purple eyes focused when she asked them. The way his voice shifted, subtle but noticeable, when he explained something to her.

Sometimes she wondered whether he found as much pleasure in answering as she did in asking.

And that thought—that a being as vast and ancient as he seemed might take enjoyment in her curiosity—made her feel both powerful and impossibly small at the same time.

Lyssena stepped closer, peering up at him through the shadowed eyes of her mask.

"You watched me the whole time," she added, blinking her eyelashes at him, though through the mask he probably couldn't see them.

"I will never be bored with you, Lyssena," her god answered her, and she smiled widely at that. Lyssena felt her chest flutter, her cheeks warm, and the need to hug him as hard as she could.

She was not yet certain whether that realization should comfort her or unsettle her all over again.

Chapter Twenty-Seven

He Was Already There

Erevos

Erevos felt a flicker of sweetness, particularly between Lyssena's legs.

Now that her entire body was covered in him, he realized that human females likely possessed what female hertas did—a hole meant to receive. For some reason, that thought had never crossed his mind before. His songbird could probably feel pleasure just as he could. That realization filled him with joy.

"What if I stay here for ten years?" Lyssena asked, and Erevos answered by baring his impressive rows of sharp teeth. He had already decided she would remain here forever.

Not ten years, not a hundred, not a thousand.

Forever.

Erevos intended to keep his songbird at his side for eternity.

"I have known you for twenty years," he said, and after remaining still for a long moment, he finally took a step toward her. "I was never bored knowing you."

Now they stood face to face.

It amused him that she only reached beneath his chest, that he had to bend his head in order to look into her eyes, eyes that searched him so openly.

"Twenty?"

"Since the day you learned to pray."

When Lyssena celebrated her third year in the human realm, her parents brought her to the temple where their people prayed each day without fail. She could not yet speak as they did, but she already knew fragments of the prayers.

That day, in the fifth month of the year, when the blooms opened brightest, and the air carried the heavy sweetness of nectar, Lyssena prayed to the god with no name.

Perhaps she did not understand that she was forbidden from doing so. Or perhaps she already understood mischief.

At the end of her prayer, after her parents had bowed their heads, Lyssena leaned closer to the altar and whispered that the god with no name should try honey.

And he did.

Erevos tried honey from a honeycomb he found in the far meadow near her village, tearing it open and letting the golden substance spill slowly over his tongue. He did not like the taste. It was bitter, thick, and clinging, coating his tongue in a way that lingered longer than it should have.

Unsatisfied, he went farther to other villages, to distant cities, to countries and continents across the world.

He sought out every variety of honey he could find—pale and translucent, dark as amber, nearly black and slow as sap— and tasted each one.

They were all the same.

So he returned to the little human.

He found her sitting in the soft grass outside her family's dwelling, legs folded beneath her, eating the very same honey he had tried—but spread generously over warm bread, the crust still dusted with flour. It glistened in the light as she lifted it to her mouth, and when she bit into it, her small face brightened as though she were tasting something delicious.

Erevos was a curious demon, and he could not understand why she would enjoy something he found bitter. Yet she did.

And that alone made it worthy of further study—at first. His curiosity grew stronger as he tried to understand not only why Lyssena enjoyed honey but also the reason for her bravery.

No human has ever spoken to him. No human has ever mentioned his name.

From that day onward, he watched Lyssena grow. He watched her limbs lengthen and her voice steady. He watched the softness of childhood become awareness. He listened as her prayers deepened, no longer mere imitation of her parents' words, but richer and warmer.

Her devotion changed as she grew. It became stronger. *Sweeter.*

She never prayed to him again after that first forbidden whisper until the day he revealed himself to her.

And when she finally did, lifting her voice to the god with no name once more, he was already there.

He had always been there.

Lyssena was quieter than usual when they began the walk back home.

She kept her gaze fixed ahead, focusing on a single direction, placing one foot in front of the other as though the act of walking required all of her attention.

When they entered the cave again, with its endless twists and slow, curving turns, Lyssena still had not spoken a word.

Erevos did not enjoy that.

It was not the comfortable silence they shared before. This silence felt different. Tighter.

He tried to determine whether something he had said had unsettled her. Had she not wished to stay? The possibility held unpleasantly against his thoughts.

He searched for any other reason his songbird would withhold her voice from him. He did not sense anger radiating from her, and he knew well how anger appeared upon her.

Lyssena rarely became upset. But when she did, it was . . . unpleasant.

He remembered the day the neighbor's chicken had leaped over the low fence and devoured the wheat Lyssena had planted, wheat she had prayed over for a good harvest, offering devotion to her nonexistent god. She had stood very still when she noticed the damage; her jaw was tight, her silence sharp as his claws.

Later that afternoon, Erevos had killed the chicken and placed its limp body upon her family's porch.

And later that night, Lyssena had eaten it before going to bed.

That memory made Erevos thoughtful.

But before he could reach any conclusion, he noticed that his Lyssena had begun walking faster. Because her steps were far smaller than his, the quickening of her pace was almost a run. She moved ahead of him without hesitation and nearly turned down the wrong passage within the cavern's winding maze.

Erevos corrected her gently by stepping into the path she was about to take, his body blocking the narrow turn without force and without a word.

At that, she pouted for the briefest moment before continuing forward in the right direction.

When they arrived at the double doors, Lyssena reached for the handles and attempted to pull them open, but they did not yield.

Erevos did not move to assist her. He wanted his songbird to grow accustomed to wielding his shadows, to remember that what belonged to him now bent toward her as well. So he waited for her to recall that she no longer needed to rely on human strength alone.

Lyssena turned to look at him, her masked green eyes staying on his for a breath as though searching for instruction, then faced the doors once more.

This time, she leaned her beak lightly against the cool surface and whispered for them to open.

And they did.

The doors parted without resistance, shadows slipping between the seams, and Erevos felt a slow bloom of pride unfurl within him as he watched her step forward. His songbird was learning. She was growing accustomed to the world that had always been his. But was now, in part, hers as well.

He still did not enjoy the unhappiness he sensed around her. Yet perhaps, he reasoned, after he fed her something warm and rich, something that would settle comfortably in her human body, she would tell him what troubled her.

Lyssena stepped inside, and Erevos followed.

"Lyssena?" he called as she turned toward her chamber.

"Yes?" She paused mid-step and half-turned to face him.

"Would you like roasted deer?"

"Yes . . . please," she murmured. When she reached her door, she opened it slowly, hesitating just slightly on the threshold, and added in a quieter voice, "Thank you," before slipping inside and closing it behind her.

Erevos remained where he stood for a moment longer, staring at the closed door.

Was it about him knowing her for so long? He could not understand why that would be a bad thing. He did not even know whether that was the reason for her silence at all.

Food, he decided. Food will make it easier.

And with that thought, Erevos went to work.

He moved toward the kitchen, which he had mimicked from Lyssena's home, a home that was no longer hers, but had become a place of grieving, where her parents and brothers wept day and night after he had taken her away. He knew this because the restored door in her room had been made of his own shadows, and Lyssena's family had never once questioned why the wood had darkened to black.

They simply accepted it.

Erevos knew what they had done every moment Lyssena had been with him and not there.

He had considered retrieving the belongings she had left behind in her room—the small objects her hands had touched daily, the fabrics that still carried her scent—but he was uncertain. He did not know whether surrounding her with fragments of her former life would comfort her or awaken a desire to return.

And that, he could not allow.

So for now, he let his songbird grow accustomed to the world that was new to her. He wanted her to like him.

To *choose* to stay with *him*.

Erevos passed the long counters and the tall pantry shelves, the large wooden table in the corner of the kitchen, and made his way to the concealed chamber beyond, the hidden room where he kept a deer alive for the sole purpose of slaughtering it fresh for Lyssena.

He had claws to tear through flesh and sinew.

And he had shadows he knew how to coax into flame.

When he passed through the wall to where the deer lay sleeping, he felt something shift.

His songbird was removing the shadows from herself.

She lifted the mask first, peeling it away from her face, and then asked the suit to loosen and reshape itself into a dress once more. Erevos felt all of it.

As he wrapped his hand around the deer's neck, preparing to snap it cleanly, he felt something else, a gentle caress along the threads of his shadows.

Lyssena was touching the feathers of her mask.

She stroked them lightly, and he felt every movement.

Chapter Twenty-Eight

Lavish and Unseen

Lyssena

The feathers were soft, and for some reason, very, very warm.

But that was the least of Lyssena's concerns.

She did not know how she felt. Whether it was anger, or violation, or something else entirely. That uncertainty was what unsettled her most.

Her god—who insisted he was not a god—had just told her that he had been watching her for nearly her entire life. She did not know how to feel about that at all.

She had been taught that gods were everywhere at once, that they saw all things without needing to choose where to look, though her god claimed those gods were not real. Yet after standing face to face with Erevos, after seeing the impossible shape of him and feeling the weight of his presence, it was difficult to accept that he had known her specifically, intentionally, all that time.

One more thing, however, stood out to Lyssena.

Erevos had said he had known her for twenty years. He had not phrased it exactly like that, but Lyssena could do simple math, and if she was twenty-three, and he had known her for twenty years, then that meant he had first seen her when she was barely more than a toddler.

What had happened then?

She could not answer that question, of course. No one remembered anything clearly from that age, and the fact that there was a gap—a stretch of her life that belonged more to him than to her memory—made her chest tighten with frustration. Tears welled in Lyssena's eyes.

She sat on her lavish bed, rubbing her eyes in her equally lavish gown, and stared at the equally lavish crown resting upon the matching drawer across the room.

Lavish. Everything was lavish now.

As she placed her new mask beside the crown, she wondered whether this abundance—this comfort, this indulgence—had made her blind to something she should have noticed sooner.

Lyssena considered Erevos good.

At first, that conclusion had been simple: he was a god, and gods were not meant to be bad.

But then again, the other gods had never listened to her prayers, not even when she had never lied, never sinned, never allowed herself to stray from the narrow path laid before her. They had remained silent.

Erevos had not.

She was confused but also thinking more deeply than she ever had before.

Erevos was good because . . . well, for one, he had saved her from an abusive husband. He had shown her the true faces of those who had betrayed her. He had given her a life filled with wonder, a world where she could finally breathe without fear pressing against her ribs. He was gentle with her. He stopped when she felt uncomfortable. He listened.

He cared.

And yet, all that thinking led her to a conclusion forming slowly in her mind. She could add another mission to her growing list.

This one would be simple in concept, though perhaps not in execution.

She would test whether her Erevos was truly good.

Lyssena did not remember when she fell asleep.

Sleep must have taken her quietly, pulling her under without dreams, because when she opened her eyes again, the first thing she noticed was the rich, mouthwatering scent of roasted meat and warm spices drifting through the air.

Her stomach rumbled painfully, and her head felt heavy. She felt terrible.

And so very hungry.

When she pushed herself upright, she moved first toward the table where a glass of water had been left waiting for her. She lifted it with eager fingers and drank greedily, finishing nearly the entire glass in one long swallow before she even paused to breathe. The coolness slid down her throat and settled into her empty stomach.

She set the cup back down and turned toward the wardrobe, still half-wondering whether more gowns would be waiting inside.

There were.

When she opened the doors, she found three more gowns hanging within, and every single one of them was made of shadow. Lyssena brushed her fingers over the material, marveling at its smoothness, at the way it yielded slightly beneath her touch, and she could not help but think that Erevos was very talented.

As far as she could tell, it might have been two days since she had left home.

Two mornings without prayer.

Two mornings without the temple.

Back in the village, every morning had begun the same way: the people gathering beneath the pale light of dawn, bowing their heads together in gratitude for whatever the gods had chosen to give them.

"What if my prayer was so strong I summoned the Greatest?" she murmured aloud, smiling at her own absurd joke before turning away and leaving the wardrobe doors open.

She still did not know how she intended to behave when she stood face to face with Erevos again.

But she knew she was hungry.

And she knew she should close the wardrobe first.

So she did, pressing the doors shut gently, and then turned toward her chamber door.

The delicious scent grew stronger with every step Lyssena took toward the kitchen, thick with roasted meat and fragrant spices that curled through the air and tickled her senses.

When she arrived, she found Erevos standing near the table, and beside him lay an entire deer, fully cooked, its body stretched across the length of the shadowy wood.

More than that, Lyssena was almost certain the table itself looked larger than it had before.

"I made you roasted deer," Erevos said, pulling out the chair nearest to him.

"I can see that."

Lyssena did not know how to react to the sight of a whole

deer. It was not merely a carved portion of it, but the entire body, legs intact, the head still attached. At least the antlers had been removed. Well, that looked . . . something.

She moved to the chair positioned opposite the one Erevos had pulled out and sat down very slowly. For a brief moment, she thought she saw his gaze sharpen at that decision—a flicker of something darker passing through his eyes—but the expression vanished almost as quickly as it came.

After another pause, this one stretching longer than the first, Erevos moved without speaking.

Lyssena swallowed.

He walked around the deer's legs protruding from the table's edge and came to stand directly behind her. She felt the warmth radiating from him immediately. A deep, consuming heat that warmed her back through the fabric of her gown, and yet, despite that warmth, a slow shiver slid down the length of her spine, followed by the faint prickling of sweat at the nape of her neck.

Erevos extended his arms to either side of her, caging her between them without ever touching her.

Lyssena watched as his right hand reached for the knife and carved a large piece of meat from the deer's flank, the blade gliding cleanly through tender flesh. With the tip of the knife, he pierced the portion and placed it onto her plate.

With his left hand, he summoned his shadows, guiding them toward the pantry to her left. The doors opened at his silent command, and two oranges slid along the dark tendrils and into his waiting palm as though delivered by invisible servants.

He squeezed the fruit into a cup, the juice running bright and fresh, and then returned to the chair he had intended to sit in from the beginning.

At that, Lyssena gulped once again.

Chapter Twenty-Nine

The God Who Killed for Flowers

Lyssena

The first bite was tender.

Lyssena chewed slowly while Erevos watched her from across the table, though his posture remained as it always did.

The meat was perfectly cooked, warm and rich with spices she had never tried, and yet she found herself focusing not on the taste but on the fact that the deer's head still rested at the center of the table, its empty eyes turned slightly toward her plate.

"This is very good," she said, smoothing her shadowy gown over her lap. "You are a great cook."

Erevos inclined his head just slightly. "You are unhappy. Why?"

Right. Erevos was not human, and Lyssena shouldn't have to run around the bush. It was difficult for her since she was always soft-spoken and never wanted to say something—anything—wrong.

She cut another piece of the soft meat, and it nearly crumbled off her knife.

"You said you have known me for twenty years," she continued, keeping her voice even, as though the question was merely a passing curiosity and not something that had followed her into sleep. "Did you watch everyone in the village . . . or only me?"

Her fingers tightened around the knife, and she kept her wrist steady.

"Only you."

The answer came without hesitation.

She lifted the cup of orange juice and took a slow sip, buying herself time, letting the silence stretch between them, because she was sweating everywhere and her heart was pounding very, very fast.

"And why me?" she asked lightly, though she did not look up from her orange juice. "There are so many people."

She placed another bite into her mouth. Across from her, Erevos still stayed unmoving. She could see him only from his chest and up, though she was still surprised she was able to see him at all, considering the giant deer across the table. But he was a tall god, or demon, or whatever he was, and he could probably see her well.

"You prayed to me."

Lyssena dabbed at the corner of her lips, though there was nothing there, and decided to play with fire.

"I was three," she said. "I also once prayed for a wooden horse to come alive."

Her gaze lifted to meet his then. "Did you plan it?" she asked. "Everything that happened after?" She did not specify what everything meant.

Her marriage, the betrayal, the timing of his appearance.

Her heartbeat had grown louder in her ears, though she kept her shoulders relaxed and her expression composed.

If he had orchestrated her suffering . . .

She cut into the meat again, though she did not immediately eat it.

Erevos's voice, when it came, was calm. "No."

Lyssena held his gaze for several seconds longer, as though weighing the word, measuring it for cracks. She finally took the bite.

The food tasted the same as before, but her throat felt tighter.

"You could have shown yourself sooner," she said after a moment, her tone softer now, less sharp but no less intentional. "If you were watching."

There it was. Not an accusation, just the shape of it.

She set her knife down and folded her hands neatly together on the table, the posture almost prayer-like without meaning to be.

"I need to know," she added, "whether you are someone who waits . . . or someone who intervenes."

Her eyes did not leave his.

And for the first time since sitting down, she allowed the silence to become heavy on purpose.

"I intervene, and I wait, Lyssena."

At the sound of her name in his voice, Lyssena felt her eyes sting as though something sharp had slipped beneath her lashes, and her skin began to crawl in a slow wave that spread from the back of her shoulders to the tips of her fingers.

She could not hold her composure any longer.

Lyssena rose abruptly from her chair and planted her trembling fists against the edge of the table, her knuckles paling as her fingers curled into the dark, shadowy wood.

"What does that even mean?"

It was the first time she had ever raised her voice. She had never—not once in her life—spoken above a measured tone to anyone, not to her parents, not to her friends, not even to those who had wronged her.

It was not a scream, nor a true shout, but the force of it vibrated through her chest and left her shaking, because the sound of her own defiance felt foreign in her mouth, and because Erevos was, after all, something far greater than a man.

"When I first began watching you," Erevos said, "it was curiosity. I wanted to understand why you delighted in honey, and what compelled you to offer it to me."

Lyssena's gaze flickered between the twin violet lights that marked his eyes, searching desperately for anything that would resemble emotion. She wished she could see his expression fully, read the language of muscle and breath.

But Erevos rarely moved at all.

He did not lean. He did not sigh. He did not click his tongue in disapproval, nor shake his head, nor let impatience show in the set of his shoulders. He simply *was*, immense and composed and impossible to decipher.

"When have I ever offered you honey?" she demanded, though her voice had dropped again.

She could not remember a single time she had offered honey to anyone. It had always been her favorite—thick and golden and clinging sweet—ever since she first tasted it when—

Oh.

On her third birthday, her mother had let her dip a small wooden spoon into a clay jar of honey, and though Lyssena could not recall the moment itself, she remembered the story repeated at family dinners, her father laughing as he told how little Lyssena had asked if they could set aside a bit of honey for the god with no name.

She had felt sorry for him.

While the other gods received prayers and offerings and praise, he received nothing at all, and in her small, earnest mind, that had seemed unbearably unfair. She had wanted to share something she loved, to make him less alone.

She remembered, too, the way the laughter had stopped. The way her mother's hand had tightened around hers. That was the day she learned it was forbidden to speak of the god with no name.

Forbidden even to wonder.

And so she had stopped.

She had stopped asking. Stopped thinking. Stopped whispering little offerings into the dark.

Not until the day her family betrayed her, until the day she stood abandoned and humiliated and alone, and there had been no one left to pray to.

No one but him.

Lyssena did not sit back down. Her fingers slowly uncurled from the edge of the table, though they still trembled, and she swallowed past the tightness in her throat before forcing the question out.

"How," she asked, her voice no longer sharp but fragile now, stretched thin with too many realizations hitting her all at once, "did you intervene?"

"In small ways," Erevos replied. "Ways that would not frighten you. Ways that allowed you to believe the world was merely . . . kind."

A chill moved across her skin at that.

"When your father opened his drawer during the winter you turned seven," he continued, "and found silver coins he did not remember earning."

Lyssena's breath caught.

That winter had been bitterly cold, the kind that crept beneath doors and through cracks in the walls, settling into bones and refusing to leave. She remembered the way her father's voice had filled the house one evening, calling her mother to the bedroom.

Coins. Several of them.

Small, dull silver pieces resting at the back of his wooden drawer, beneath folded cloth, where no one had placed them.

She remembered standing in the doorway, small and barefoot, watching her father turn the coins over and over in his rough hands, frowning as though trying to recall a memory that would not come. He had insisted he would never forget earning silver, not when money was so scarce.

But that week, they had eaten warm bread every night.

Her mother had bought thicker wool for lining their cloaks. Lyssena had been given a pale blue ribbon, which she had worn in her hair until it frayed.

She had thought it a miracle. She had thought perhaps the gods had finally answered.

"I placed them there," Erevos said simply.

Her stomach twisted.

"There were other times," he continued, "When your grains were eaten before harvest. When your flowers were trampled."

Lyssena's lips parted slightly. She remembered that, too.

The small patch of land behind their house had been her mother's pride—rows of modest vegetables, delicate flowers lining the fence—and there had been seasons when animals broke through. Chickens from neighboring yards scratching through their grains. Pigs nosing beneath the fence and crushing blossoms beneath blunt hooves.

And yet . . .

There had been evenings when her father would return home carrying meat.

Not the thin broth they were used to, but proper meat.

Roasted chicken, crisped at the edges, the skin blistered and fragrant. Pork slow-cooked with herbs, the scent filled the entire house and made Lyssena dizzy with hunger before she even sat down.

She remembered how her mother would murmur that it was fortunate, so fortunate, that one of the neighbor's animals had fallen ill, that it would have gone to waste otherwise.

Lyssena had eaten with sticky fingers and shining eyes.

"I killed them," Erevos said, his words were not boastful or cruel. Simply factual. "Every chicken that devoured what you planted. Every pig that uprooted what you tended."

Her breath came slower now.

"You were fond of the yellow flowers by the fence," he added. "You cried when they were crushed."

She had, and she had forgotten that. But now she could see herself kneeling in the dirt, small fingers trying to press broken stems back into the soil, her vision blurred with tears while her mother told her that some things did not grow back once ruined.

A strange warmth began to spread through her chest, confusing and overwhelming. All those moments she had believed to be chance. All those tiny mercies.

"You . . . did that for me?" she whispered.

"For you," he answered.

Not for her family, for *her*. And he never asked for a single prayer or a gift.

Lyssena's anger, which had burned so fiercely only moments before, began to soften, melting into something tender and aching and impossibly intimate.

He had watched her delight in honey.

He had noticed her tears over flowers.

He had known the rhythm of her household well enough to slip coins into a drawer without being seen.

He had been there.

Through winters and harvests and small birthdays and disappointments.

Always there.

"You were . . . kind," she said at last, the words trembling as they left her mouth.

She did not know whether she meant to accuse him or thank him. What kind of being memorized the things that made her smile? What kind of being killed for her flowers?

And yet . . . What kind of being did all that and never asked for anything in return?

Lyssena lowered herself back into her chair without breaking eye contact, her pulse no longer racing in fear but in something softer.

"You were taking care of me," she murmured.

And for the first time since the conversation began, her voice held no edge at all.

Chapter Thirty

The Bloom Beneath His Chest

Erevos

"I will always take care of you. I will always choose you, and my greatest desire is for you to choose me in return," Erevos said, watching as a single tear gathered at the corner of his songbird's eye, trembling there like a fragile jewel that did not yet know whether to fall.

He did not fully understand why she wept.

He understood sorrow when it was harvested, fear when it was tasted, devotion when it was offered in trembling prayer, but this sharp and luminous grief born from his promise was something unfamiliar, something that did not resemble the emotions he had consumed for centuries. And yet he knew that she was his whole existence.

Before Lyssena, he had not been interested in anything at all.

He had existed as other demons existed, vast and patient and hollow, harvesting emotions from mortals the way storms harvested leaves, not out of cruelty nor kindness, but because

"

that was the nature of their being. He had drifted through centuries untouched by pain, untouched by longing, untouched by the ache that now lived beneath his ribs.

Lyssena had given him meaning.

She had given him devotion without realizing she had done so, had offered him her whispered prayers and her fairness and her stubborn hope, and those small, radiant things had become the sweetest gifts he had ever known.

He had waited twenty years for her to choose him.

Twenty years of watching, of restraining himself, of placing coins in drawers and blood upon the soil in offerings of protection.

And she had chosen him.

She had spoken his name into the dark when she believed herself abandoned, had prayed for him to come when he had already been there, waiting with infinite patience for the sound of her voice to claim him.

Her tear slipped free, then another, tracing the curve of her cheeks, and Erevos felt something disturbingly close to guilt. A tightening, a pressure that seemed to gather at the center of his chest. She wept because of his words.

And that pained him. Erevos physically felt pain.

His gaze dropped slowly to his chest, and he lifted one clawed hand to the place, dragging the tips of his fingers lightly over the shadowed surface of his form as if he might carve the discomfort out and examine it. He had never felt such a thing before.

Not in centuries of existence.

"I'm so sorry!" Lyssena cried, her voice breaking as the tears fell faster, and each drop that struck his shadows dissolved into him like warm rain, and he felt them, every single one, as though her sorrow were imprinting itself upon his very essence.

Erevos rose immediately from his seat. The movement was driven by something far more primal than thought.

He stepped toward her, and before he could reach her fully, she had already turned toward him, her body angling in his direction as though drawn by an invisible ribbon that bound them together.

When he lowered himself, preparing to gather her into his arms, she lifted hers first.

That, more than her tears, more than her words, filled him with something so vast it eclipsed the pain in his chest entirely. *Joy.*

It surged through him like a tide breaking against ancient stone, warm and consuming and unbearably bright, and for a moment, he could not distinguish where his shadows ended, and that feeling began.

She wanted him. She reached for him.

His songbird now stretched her arms toward him without hesitation. Erevos folded her against his chest, enclosing her within the vastness of his form, his claws curving protectively around her back as though shielding a flame from the wind.

He was glad.

Glad beyond reason. Glad that she sought his closeness again. Glad that her tears did not drive her away. Glad that, after twenty years of waiting, she still chose to step into his embrace.

Lyssena did not hesitate once she was within his arms; she moved closer.

Not merely resting against him, not merely accepting the shelter he offered, but *seeking* him. Her fingers curling into the dark substance of his form as though testing whether he was solid enough to hold her, her forehead brushing against his jaw before she turned her face and nuzzled into him with a small, trembling sigh. The sound alone undid him.

Erevos had known hunger.

He had known satisfaction.

He had known the distant, muted pleasure of consuming emotions from afar.

But this warmth that unfurled slowly inside him as she burrowed against his neck was something entirely different. The warmth inside him expanded.

It spread through him slowly like ink dissolving into clear water, filling spaces he had not known were empty. The shadows composing his form stirred. He felt . . . full.

And warm.

The warmth was unfamiliar and yet not, because he had felt echoes of it before, always when Lyssena stood near him, always when her hand brushed against his shadows, always when she spoke to him in that quiet, earnest way that belonged only to her.

But now it was stronger, and now it bloomed.

The sensation gathered at the center of him and opened outward, petal by petal, as though some ancient and dormant thing within his being had decided at last to awaken.

His claws flexed gently against her back, careful, so careful, as though she were made of glass and breath and something far more fragile than mortal flesh.

She nuzzled him again, and Erevos felt the bloom deepen.

Lyssena slowly pulled back just enough to lift her hands to her face, brushing at her damp cheeks with the heels of her palms, her lashes still clumped together from tears. She sniffed once. A single tear clung stubbornly to the curve of her cheek.

Erevos watched it.

He did not understand why he watched it, only that he wanted to.

He lowered his head, drawn by need rather than reason,

and before she could brush it away, he extended his tongue, tasting the salt of her grief directly from her skin.

Lyssena gasped. The sound was sharp and startled and delightful.

"You have a tongue!"

Erevos stilled.

Slowly, he withdrew, studying her wide eyes as though she had just revealed something deeply perplexing.

"Why would I not?" he asked, genuine confusion threading through his ancient voice.

She stared at him, her lips parted, her cheeks flushing into a deeper shade of pink beneath the remnants of her tears.

"I don't know," she breathed. "You're . . . you."

"I speak," he said after a moment, as though explaining something obvious to a child. "Speech requires a tongue."

Lyssena blinked at that. "I never saw it."

"You did not look inside my mouth."

Her breath hitched again, though this time for an entirely different reason.

The blooming inside him intensified at the change in her scent, at the subtle shift in her pulse beneath his hands. The warmth coiled lower within his body, less innocent, less purely tender.

"I did not think you would . . . taste things," she murmured.

Erevos considered that. "I taste many things," he replied. "Fear, devotion, desire." His gaze lowered to her lips. "And now," he added, quieter, "I have tasted your sorrow."

Lyssena swallowed. "They were only tears."

"They were yours."

That seemed to affect her more than anything else he had said, because now she smelled sweet again.

A silence stretched between them. Lyssena's fingers curled once more into his shadows, but this time the gesture was slower, exploratory even. She studied him openly, curiosity took hold of her thoughts, and there was something almost playful in the way her gaze danced over his face.

"So you do have a tongue," she said again, as though confirming a fascinating discovery.

Erevos's shadows shifted behind him. "Yes."

"And teeth."

"Yes."

"Many of them."

"More than you do, so to you it is many."

Her breath left her in a slow exhale. "And you used neither on me."

The bloom inside him turned molten at that. Also, his little songbird was completely pink, red even.

"I would not harm you," he said, feeling his spikes twitch at her comment.

Lyssena did not look afraid.

If anything, she leaned closer again, her forehead brushing against his chin.

"I know," she whispered.

And Erevos realized only now that she trusted him. He also felt her breath on his skin and heat between his legs.

Chapter Thirty-One

What the Deer Witnessed

Lyssena

Out of all the scandalous things she could have said, she had chosen to remark that her Erevos had not yet tried his tongue and teeth on her.

It was wildly inappropriate. It was shameless.

And the fact that the words had left her mouth so easily made heat creep slowly up her throat and settle in her cheeks.

But she was his songbird, and he was her god, and now she was certain that he was a good one.

Strangely, that certainty allowed her lungs to fill more deeply than they had in days. Even though the knowledge that he had watched her for most of her life should have been unsettling, should have sent her fleeing in horror, it did not root fear inside her the way it would have if he had been human. If he were human, she would have run. If he were human, she would have felt hunted.

But Erevos was not human at all, and she found that she liked that very much.

He did not carry the same narrow mindsets men did, did not measure her behavior against invisible social rules, or expect her to perform softness in precise and suffocating ways. The fragile structures she had lived by her entire life—speak gently, sit properly, never desire openly, never embarrass yourself—seemed to dissolve in his presence like mist burned away by the sun.

No matter how many times she stumbled over her words, no matter how bold or absurd or improper she sounded, Erevos never laughed, never recoiled, never judged.

He simply watched her.

And chose her.

Lyssena realized that what she cherished most was not merely his protection, but the way she felt in his presence. Lyssena felt comfortable.

He was kind and attentive. He was patient. And he was not bound by the limitations of mortal men.

She found herself thinking not only about the things he had done *for* her, but about what he *was*.

That otherworldly male. That ancient, towering being of shadow and violet light.

She did not know how much time had passed since she had first stepped into this place with him, since her world had cracked open and rearranged itself entirely, but as she stood there within his arms, she felt . . . content.

"Where," Erevos asked, his voice low and thoughtful, "may I use my tongue and teeth?"

Lyssena's breath faltered. She had not yet recovered from her own boldness, and now his question slid over her skin like warm silk, settling low in her body.

Heat bloomed between her thighs, a slow spreading warmth that made her knees feel weaker. Her pulse began to thrum in places she had been taught never to acknowledge, and she became acutely aware of the way her gown brushed against her hips, the way the air shifted when he moved even slightly closer. Lyssena swallowed.

She was aroused.

Her body had responded before her mind could compose something proper and restrained, and the damp heat gathering in her most intimate place made her inhale sharply through her nose as though she might steady herself through sheer will.

He was watching her. Of course he was.

He always watched her.

And the thought that he might notice only made the warmth deepen.

Lyssena lifted her gaze slowly to meet the twin violet lights of his eyes, and though her cheeks were flushed and her lips parted with uneven breath, she did not retreat.

"You truly do not know?" she asked softly, though her voice trembled at the edges.

Because if he did not . . .

If this ancient being of shadow truly did not understand what he was asking . . .

Then she would have to show him. And the thought of that made her pulse stutter all over again.

Her mother had once told her that when a woman wed, she must please her husband with her mouth, that it was her duty to kneel if asked, and that if she were fortunate—if she were very fortunate—the man might one day decide to return the favor. It had been spoken like a secret, a transaction. Like something endured.

Her voice dropped to a murmur, soft and almost shy despite the boldness of the words.

"You could . . . " She hesitated, her breath trembling. "You could place your mouth . . . on me."

Erevos hummed. The sound vibrated low in his chest, and

before she could gather another breath, the table behind her seemed to lengthen slightly, or perhaps it was only her perception bending under the weight of what was happening, because in the next moment Erevos moved her as though she weighed nothing at all and set her upon the dark wood.

Lyssena gasped as her palms pressed against the surface for balance.

She was suddenly aware of the deer's head mere inches from her, its empty eyes staring eternally forward.

Erevos stepped between her knees.

He leaned forward, placing both hands on the table at either side of her hips, caging her in without touching her, his vast body towering over her as shadows pooled and curled around the edges of the wood.

Lyssena's breath grew shallow.

She could feel how wet she was now, embarrassingly soaked, the fabric of her undergarments clinging to her with every tiny shift of her hips. Her thighs pressed together, only to part again when Erevos moved closer.

"I have never done this," she admitted, her voice barely more than a breath, her fingers curling into the table's edge.

Erevos's gaze darkened, and Lyssena had not expected that at all.

"Nor have I," he replied, his tone unashamed. "But I wish to."

The simplicity of it made her stomach flip. The shadows beneath her stirred, and her gown began to lift.

The fabric slid upward along her legs as though guided by unseen hands, exposing inch after inch of warm, flushed skin to the cool air of the kitchen. Lyssena's breath hitched sharply as the hem rose above her knees, then higher still, pooling around her hips like spilled ink.

"Erevos—" she whispered, though she did not wish for him to stop. She was shy, but also eager, and so very curious.

Erevos lifted his hand from the table, and Lyssena followed his movement. His arm was as thick as her thigh, and Lyssena was a proud woman, with plump thighs to hold her generous arse.

Her gaze traveled along his wrist as it slowly got closer and closer to her skin.

The contrast between shadow and touch made her blink.

He slid his palm upward, the pads of his fingers grazing along the sensitive inside of her thigh, leaving heat along her skin. Her muscles trembled under his touch, instinctively wanting to close, to hide, yet opening for him instead.

He reached the curve where her thigh met her hip and paused, his thumb pressing lightly into the softness there as though memorizing the shape of her.

"You are warm," he murmured, and it was the first time she noticed that Erevos's gaze was unfocused.

Lyssena's breathing had grown heavy now, uneven and almost desperate, each inhale catching halfway in her chest before spilling out in a shaky exhale. Her fingers tightened against the table, her back arching just slightly as though drawn upward by invisible strings.

"Yes," she breathed, her voice thin. "I— I think I am."

Erevos tilted his head, studying her.

Her second thigh lifted gently under his guiding hand, her leg parting wider for him, and the air against her most intimate place made her shudder visibly.

She could feel how exposed she was, how vulnerable.

How utterly ready.

Her heart pounded so loudly she wondered if he could hear it. Perhaps he could.

Because his gaze darkened, and he leaned closer.

Chapter Thirty-Two

The First Wound

Erevos

E revos had believed he understood hunger.

He had existed on it. For centuries, he had harvested emotions without preference, consuming them as easily as breathing. But this . . . This was ruinous.

Lyssena's scent rolled off her in waves so thick he could taste it in the air, could feel it dissolving into his shadows, could feel it sinking into him like molten gold poured into hollow spaces. Her nervousness, her anticipation, the fragile tremor of trust beneath it all—it was overwhelming.

He was drinking without meaning to, and it made focusing nearly impossible.

She sat exposed before him, breath uneven, thighs parted by his hands, and for the first time in his long existence, Erevos understood distraction.

"Lyssena," he said, his hand remaining on her leg. He wanted to touch every organ of her body. His songbird was just too soft.

Erevos's shadows trembled around them, and his cock grew heavy.

It strained forward, brushing against the edge of the table as he leaned closer; the pressure felt too good. The sensation was foreign and distracting and almost maddening.

He shifted his weight. Just slightly.

His thighs moved in a restrained, slow, back and forth against the wood, seeking relief without abandoning his focus, friction sending flickers of sensation through him that only sharpened the hunger pooling at the center of his being.

Lyssena inhaled sharply at the movement, and he saw the way her gaze flickered downward. Saw the flush deepen along her neck.

Erevos drew his tongue slowly over his teeth, tasting the air between them, tasting her.

Her scent had changed. It was richer now, and so much warmer.

It was inviting.

"You are . . . intoxicating," he said, his voice lower than before, threaded with something rougher, something no longer composed.

Her emotions tangled and untangled at that, and he swallowed them instinctively. He had imagined touching her countless times in the privacy of his own thoughts. Imagined the softness of her, the way her body would respond, the sounds she might make.

But imagination had not prepared him for reality. For the tremble of her thighs beneath his hand. For the way her breath stuttered when his thumb moved a fraction lower.

For the sight of her exposed like this, trusting him, offering herself to the god with no name.

He leaned closer, lowering himself until his face hovered

near the heat of her, violet gaze lifting briefly to meet hers, and his knees met the floor.

She was watching him, wide-eyed. Flushed and breathing hard.

And entirely *his*.

I will be gentle, he thought as his gaze lowered back to the curls between his songbird's legs.

His jaw tightened as he felt her scent, and his tongue glided against the back of his teeth.

None of it would be gentle; Erevos was starving.

Erevos nearly asked her what he was meant to do.

The question hovered at the edge of his thoughts, and yet here, before the soft, trembling heat of her body, he felt inexperienced in a way that both unsettled and thrilled him.

But the impulse faded as quickly as it came, because Erevos wished to discover everything all by himself.

Slowly, he opened his jaw, stretching it wider than any mortal man's could manage, his long, thick tongue sliding forward between sharpened teeth as shadows moved around him. He did not hesitate.

He lowered himself the final inch and dragged his tongue over Lyssena's most intimate place, over the part of her she had never shown him.

His songbird released a high, broken sound at the first slow stroke of his tongue against her skin, a sound so soft and unguarded that his shadows shuddered violently around them. His hunger flared.

He had thought her scent overwhelming.

He had believed nothing could surpass the sweetness of her devotion, the golden ache of her trust as he fed upon it. And oh, he had been wrong.

Her skin was warmer, softer than anything he had ever

touched, and the taste of her made something tighten deep within him.

A growl rumbled low in his chest as he pressed closer, flattening his tongue and sliding it deeper between the folds Lyssena carried, parting her gently at first, then more firmly as instinct overtook anything else.

"Erevos!" she cried, her voice fracturing into breath and need as his tongue brushed over a small swell hidden between her folds. He felt it beneath the broad stroke of his tongue.

What was it? He did not know.

But he knew it made her tremble, he knew it made her say his name.

For the first time, she called him like that, and the sound fed him more fiercely than devotion ever had.

A dark, possessive pride unfurled inside him, and he circled the small swell again, slower, testing the pressure, watching the way her thighs quivered, the way her hips lifted helplessly toward his mouth as though her body itself begged for more.

He was intoxicated by everything. The heat of her against his tongue, the wetness growing with each stroke, the scent thickening in the air until it clung to him like a second skin.

The more he tasted her, the wetter his Lyssena became.

Her arousal coated his mouth, smeared along his chin, and glistened against the shadows that curled eagerly along his jaw.

He wanted more. He wanted to push deeper, to pry her open and drink from her until she shattered beneath him while her cries became louder and louder.

Erevos wanted to drown in it.

In her.

In the endless, exquisite proof that his songbird responded to him, that he, who had once believed himself sustained solely by emotion, could now hunger for flesh.

He dragged his tongue slowly downward through her folds, parting her. *There.*

A small entrance, hidden beneath warmth and wetness, softer than the surrounding flesh and clenched as though guarding something within. His shadows stilled.

So he had been right.

His songbird did possess a place meant to be entered.

The discovery sent a pulse of dark satisfaction through him, and without fully understanding why his hunger sharpened so suddenly, Erevos pressed the tip of his tongue against that tight opening and nudged forward.

He expected her to cry out again in pleasure.

Expected her hips to lift the way they had when he circled the sensitive swell above.

Instead, the moment the thick tip of his tongue breached her entrance and slid even a fraction inside, Lyssena let out a loud, broken whimper, her thighs snapping shut around his head with startling force. Erevos froze instantly.

His shadows recoiled violently from the table's surface, flaring outward in alarm as he withdrew at once, lifting his head, his gaze flashing upward to her face.

"Lyssena," he said, "did I wound you?"

Her breathing was ragged, her fingers clenched tight against the wood, her chest rising and falling in uneven pulls as she forced her thighs to loosen around him, though her entire body trembled.

"It—" she tried, her voice thin, breath catching. "It hurt."

Hurt . . . He had meant to bring her pleasure.

A low, unstable growl rolled through his chest, not at her, but at himself, at his own ignorance, his own failure to understand the fragility of her human body.

"I will not continue," he said at once, beginning to rise, shadows thickening as though preparing to pull her away from the table entirely, to shield her from further harm. "I apologize."

But Lyssena reached for him, gently placing her hand on his.

"It is normal," she breathed, her cheeks flushed, her voice shy yet steadying. "The first time . . . it hurts. My mother said so."

"You are certain?" he asked.

Lyssena swallowed, her thighs parting again, though more hesitantly this time.

"Yes," she whispered. "Just . . . go slowly."

Erevos inclined his head, though inside he felt anything but slow.

He lowered himself again, his shadows settling against the table's legs to anchor him there.

Erevos traced downward from the swelling, flattening his tongue and dragging it through the slick warmth between her folds, feeling how readily her body parted for him now, how the wet heat gathered more generously than before, coating the broad muscle of his tongue until it gleamed.

He studied the change in Lyssena's breathing as he moved. He tasted her blood while gripping her gown that was made of him. When he reached her entrance once more, he did not press immediately. He lingered.

He let the tip of his tongue circle the rim, mapping its shape, feeling how it tightened in response to each touch.

So small, so guarded, so *his*.

Erevos moved slowly. He nudged forward again, gently, easing just the tip of his tongue inside, allowing her body to stretch around him rather than forcing his way through.

The inside of her was hotter than the outside, softer, more yielding, yet circled him in the way her hand did on his cock before.

He pushed a fraction deeper, and he felt her part around him.

Erevos felt the slick walls tremble and tighten before easing again, as though learning him even as he learned her.

A broken sound slipped from Lyssena's throat. It was similar to those she made when she felt good.

Encouraged, Erevos drew his tongue back slowly, feeling the way her inner walls dragged along its length, coating it more thoroughly in her arousal, and then he pressed inward again, deeper, savoring the sensation of parting her from within.

Each time he slid in and out, she released that same unsteady sound, her hips shifting against his mouth as though chasing the movement. He felt everything.

He wanted to know how deep she could take him. He wanted to see how her body changed if he altered his rhythm. So he did.

He pushed his tongue deeper, holding it there for a suspended moment, then slowly withdrew, only to thrust back in, and the reaction he earned made his shadows ripple violently across the floor. His cock pulsed between his thighs.

He had nearly forgotten he had it at all.

Another thick bead slipped from the tip, trailing down the heavy length and falling uselessly toward the floor.

Without lifting his mouth from her, Erevos summoned his shadows, feeling them coil around his shaft as they wrapped him from base to tip.

The next time he slid his tongue into her, he tightened the shadows at the same time. The combined sensation made heat run through him, his hips jerking against the restraint of his own shadows as pleasure lanced up his spine while his tongue remained buried inside his little songbird, feeling her pulse and quiver around him.

For a moment, his mind emptied entirely.

He was aware only of sensation, of the hot, silken interior of her clasping his tongue.

Of the slick sweetness coating his mouth, of the pressure of his own shadows holding him in time with the thrusting of his tongue.

Lyssena's voice grew louder now, no longer shy or startled but openly trembling, each breath spilling into another of those soft sounds that vibrated against his face. He did not understand the language of these noises.

But he understood their meaning.

And he had no desire to stop.

Chapter Thirty-Three

Eternity is Forever

Lyssena

Lyssena nearly lost her balance, and holding herself together while Erevos so nearly sent her into the next realm proved a far more difficult task than she had anticipated.

Especially since she was still perched so precariously close to that enormous deer's head, its glassy eyes forever fixed ahead as though bearing witness to her shameless behavior.

Her god's—or demon's—or Erevos's, which she truly could not bring herself to care about in that moment—tongue slid in and out of her faster and faster, and she felt every single ridge, every bump along its thick length as it parted her from within.

Erevos possessed a tongue that Lyssena would have never guessed, broad and heavy and textured, perhaps as thick as her wrist, and though it had hurt at first—so sharply she had nearly shed tears from the sting of it—now Lyssena was certain she might faint from the sheer pleasure of it.

When she felt her cunt pulsing around him, when she

noticed the heat between her thighs had grown so swollen and flushed that even the air brushing against her felt like a touch, she was certain she stood on the edge of release.

Instead, her Erevos stopped. And then he rose.

The image before her eyes was something she never thought she would witness in her life.

Erevos unfolded to his full height, forcing her to tilt her chin upward just to follow the slow withdrawal of his violet tongue from between his sharpened teeth.

She wanted to ask why he had stopped, wanted to demand it through breathless protest, but she could not form a single coherent word.

Her Erevos stood before her, his entire face glistening obscenely, her arousal tracing a wet path from the upper row of his sharp teeth to the lower, clinging to the edges as his long tongue slid outward again, licking across each shard.

"I have a cock," he said, and his mouth widened.

At that, her gaze dropped.

His cock was thick and heavy between his thighs, flushed darker at the tip, and it leaked so steadily that dark trails of demon seed had already streaked down the inside of his left leg, glistening against shadowed skin before dripping to the floor.

What a sight that was.

Lyssena forgot her manners entirely.

Forgot propriety.

Forgot the teachings of her mother and the expectations of her village.

She wanted nothing more than to feel that cock as deep inside her as her body would possibly allow, to replace the emptiness still pulsing inside her with something solid as that thick cock before her.

Her eyelids felt heavy, her breasts achingly sensitive

beneath the fabric of her gown, her nipples tightening at the mere sight of him. Lyssena wanted more.

"Please," she breathed, the word soft and trembling as it slipped past her parted lips, and in that single plea, every ounce of shame she had ever carried remained far behind in her village.

Her knees fell open wider without conscious thought, and when Erevos stepped closer, he wrapped one of his large hands firmly around her waist, anchoring her in place, while the other slid down to grasp his leaking length.

Lyssena had never imagined she could feel so unrestrained.

Erevos positioned himself closer until the heavy length of him brushed against her thigh, and for a moment, he only looked at her, his gaze darker than she had ever seen it, as though he were still deciding how best to consume her. For her, any way he'd choose would be great.

"I believed," he began slowly, his voice thick, "that this was meant for your mouth."

His hand shifted along his cock as he spoke, stroking once.

"You placed your hand around me before," he continued, tilting his head slightly, "and I assumed perhaps your mouth was another place for it."

Lyssena swallowed.

"But then I learned," he said, stepping even closer between her parted thighs, the tip of him pressing tentatively against her swollen entrance, "that you possess a place meant to receive."

His gaze lifted to hers. "As you received my tongue."

Heat burned across her face at the bluntness of it, but she did not retreat. In fact, Lyssena never wanted him to stop talking.

Erevos lowered his eyes to where they joined and guided himself carefully, the thick tip nudging against her with a slow, testing pressure that made her inhale sharply.

He did not thrust.

He pressed. Gradually.

Lyssena felt the stretch deeper than before, more solid, and when the head of him breached her and slid inside, Erevos threw his head back with a loud, raw growl that shook the air around them. All of his shadows shuddered.

"It feels—" His voice faltered as he pushed another inch forward, watching her body yield around him. "It feels different from your hand."

Lyssena arched immediately, her back bowing as she gripped the edge of the table at her side.

"It—" she breathed, struggling to gather her thoughts as he filled her further, her voice breaking into uneven fragments. "We have . . . we have a long time . . . to try everything."

The words dissolved into a trembling gasp as he sank deeper.

Erevos's expression shifted at that. "Yes," he said, his tone darkening as he finally pushed fully inside her, the last of the distance closing in a slow slide that made her cry out.

"We have all the time in the world."

His hands came to her hips then, "Eternity," he added, leaning down until his forehead nearly brushed hers, "is forever."

The word eternity flickered through her mind, a question forming at the edges of her pleasure, but before she could grasp it, he moved.

The first motion was slow. Lyssena felt his hips brushing against her skin, then she felt the slow withdrawal that left her feeling suddenly empty.

Erevos pressed forward again, deeper, firmer, the friction drawing a strained sound from her throat as pain and pleasure tangled tightly together.

It hurt, but she loved it.

She loved the way he watched her face as he moved, pumping into her again and again. She loved the way he held her, as though determined not to let her slip away.

The rhythm built gradually, his restraint thinning as the sensation overtook him. His movements growing stronger, faster, the table shifting faintly beneath them with each thrust.

He lifted her slightly, sliding her more fully onto him until her body arched and her hips tilted upward, her weight balanced in his grasp, and the new angle made her cry out louder, her nails scraping along the wood behind her.

He moved her with him then—guiding her back and forth along his length—until the world blurred at the edges of her sight.

Her pleasure rose fast, cresting before she could prepare for it, her body tightening around him as she gasped his name in broken syllables, her release tearing through her in a wave so intense it left her trembling in his hands.

Erevos stilled for only a fraction of a second, then he groaned low and rough, burying himself fully within her as his own release followed, heat spilling deep as his shadows flared violently around the room.

For a moment, neither of them moved.

Lyssena sagged against him, breathless and dizzy, trying her best to hold on to him.

Erevos held her there, as though he had claimed not merely her body, but the future she did not yet know awaited her.

Chapter Thirty-Four

To Kiss a Demon

Erevos

For a long moment after their bodies stilled, Erevos did not move.

Lyssena remained on his cock, her arms loose on his torso, her breath shallow and spent against his chest, and he was acutely aware of every place where they were still joined, of the warmth enclosing him, of the pulse inside her that had not yet settled.

He felt . . . different. Full.

When he finally moved, easing his hands more securely beneath her thighs, he lifted her slowly, and the motion caused his still semi-hardened cock to slide free of her body with a slow, slick withdrawal that drew a sensitive tremor through them both.

Erevos watched the place where they separated. Her body released him reluctantly, and a thick trail of his seed followed after, spilling down the inside of her thigh in dark streaks that glistened against her flushed skin.

He stared.

Demons did not reproduce. They did not spill seed, and yet he had.

He adjusted his hold on her, cradling her closer against his chest. Lyssena's head rested just beneath his chin, her hair damp at the temples, her lashes heavy as she looked up at him with that soft, open gaze that made something inside his chest grow unbearably warm. He had barely cooled from their mating, and already that look burned heat through him again.

"Erevos," she murmured, her voice faint and breath-warmed, "do you . . . want to kiss?"

The question caught him off guard. "Kiss," he repeated.

She nodded, her expression turning shy. "I have never done it before," she admitted, her fingers curling lightly against his chest. "But I think I would like to try."

Her gaze flickered to his mouth, or rather, to the sharp rows of teeth that filled it.

"I am only . . . uncertain," she added, "because you have so many of those."

Erevos had devoured fear with those teeth. Therefore, he had never considered them an obstacle.

"How," he asked, his voice gentler than its usual timbre, "should I kiss you?"

Lyssena hesitated, then lifted both hands slowly and placed them on his face; her palms were warm against the shadowed planes of him. Her touch alone made him still.

She studied him, her green eyes dancing between his, and then—with a small inhale—she leaned forward and pressed her mouth to the space just below his teeth, where his lips would have rested if he had any. The contact was light. It was warm, and it lasted a second.

It was not violent. It was . . . delicate.

When Lyssena pulled back, Erevos was unsure what had just happened.

"I want to understand," he said at last, his tone solemn despite the bloom beginning to spread through him.

Her brows lifted.

"Again," he clarified, leaning down to her face.

A small smile curved her mouth, and she pressed her lips to him once more, this time lingering a fraction longer, her fingers tightening against his jaw as though testing whether he might bite.

He did not.

He only absorbed the sensation, the softness, the warmth, the faint taste of her breath.

When she withdrew, she let out a small, breathy giggle. Warmth bloomed through him all over again, curling through his shadows until they shifted around them like a living embrace.

Erevos tightened his hold on her just enough not to restrain, only enough to ensure she remained exactly where she was. He did not yet understand kissing or the fluid he had spilled.

But he understood that he wanted to learn everything with her.

"I think it may be time to clean up," Lyssena said.

"Yes," he agreed at once.

He brushed her hair away from her forehead and carried her from the kitchen, his feet making no sound against the shadow-formed floor.

The hallway beyond was almost done. While his songbird slept, Erevos tended to the house. His current project was the breaks on the walls. He wanted to make them even and to have Lyssena enjoy the decoration and texture, rather than empty surfaces. Soon, the house would be complete, and it would be worthy of her.

He glanced down at Lyssena, imagining her wandering these halls, choosing fabrics and shapes, imprinting herself into every dark corner until the place bore her mark as much as his.

The thought brought him joy.

When they reached the end of the corridor, he nudged open the door to the bathing chamber, where the water he created stayed warm and steamy.

Lyssena shifted in his arms. "I need to . . . relieve myself first," she admitted, her cheeks pinking despite everything they had just done.

He carried her directly to the waste pot tucked near the far wall and set her upon it.

Lyssena blinked up at him. "I am not a child," she said, looking at the pot, then back at him. "I can do that myself."

"I am aware," he replied.

She paused. "Then why did you carry me to it?"

"You are required to be placed upon it," he said. "You are tired."

Lyssena stared at him for a long moment, then huffed a faint breath. "That does not mean you must supervise."

"I am not supervising," he countered, folding his arms as he remained exactly where he was. "I am observing."

Her lips twitched despite herself. "Unbelievable."

"And yet," he said, "you remain seated."

She tried—and failed—to suppress a smile before shaking her head and lifting the hem of her gown out of the way.

When she settled properly onto the pot and finally relaxed enough to let go, a soft sound filled the quiet chamber, and almost immediately she winced.

Erevos straightened.

Pain flickered across her face, and his shadows sharpened instinctively along the floor.

"It burns," she admitted through a small exhale, her brows drawing together.

His gaze darkened. "Why?"

"My mother told me it might," Lyssena explained, her voice steadying as she focused on breathing through her discomfort. "The first time can make everything . . . tender."

Erevos was very displeased with himself for knowing so little of mating and its consequences. He had never thought he would ever experience it; he never had any interest in it. At all.

Now he knew he had to understand every piece of the process. He was a curious demon, of course.

"It is swollen," she added, gesturing vaguely between her thighs. "I will need to put medicine there. Something soothing."

"What medicine?"

"An herbal salve," she said. "There are women in my village who make it. It helps calm the skin."

His mind moved quickly through possibilities—shadow synthesis, matter shaping, reconstruction of known substances —but he realized with a great amount of irritation that he did not possess sufficient knowledge of mortal herbal combinations to recreate it accurately. He could bend shadows or fracture realms. But he did not know how to craft a village woman's soothing salve.

"I will acquire it," he said.

Lyssena blinked at him. "Acquire it?"

"I will go to your realm and retrieve this medicine," he clarified, as though stating the most obvious solution. "You require it."

She opened her mouth to protest, then closed it again. She was too tired to argue with a demon-god who treated inter-realm travel like walking into another room.

By the time she finished relieving herself, the initial sting had dulled slightly, though she still looked swollen and flushed.

Mortal bodies expelled waste even after ecstasy. Fascinating.

With a small motion of his hand, he bent the matter within, dissolving the liquid and its remnants into fine, harmless particles that shimmered before dispersing into the air and vanishing entirely, absorbed back into the architecture of shadow itself.

Lyssena stared.

"That is convenient," she murmured.

Erevos looked mildly pleased. "Yes."

Then he crouched before her again, his hands returning gently to her waist.

"Now," he said, his voice softer once more, "we will tend to you."

Chapter Thirty-Five

A Banquet in The Void

Lyssena

Every passing day felt better than the one before it, softer and fuller in a way Lyssena had never known life could be. Not that she truly knew how many days had passed, but by the rhythm of her sleep, by the way her body drifted into rest and woke again in his shadow-warmed bed, she guessed it had been three . . . perhaps four days.

Lyssena loved this home Erevos had created for her.

She loved its vastness, the echo of her footsteps along corridors shaped from shadow. There were rooms filled with fabrics softer than any she had touched in her village, tables carved from darkness that shimmered when she brushed her fingertips across them, alcoves glowing with dim, atmospheric light that made the walls feel alive. And she especially adored the bathing chamber.

Steam curled thick and silver through the air as she removed her beautiful gown, letting the fabric whisper down her body before she folded it carefully and rested it atop a

"

smooth, warm rock near the water's edge. The air kissed her bare skin at once, and she inhaled deeply, feeling the heat cling to her breasts, her hips, her thighs.

Lyssena was proud of her full figure, and now that she had been intimate with Erevos, she found herself swaying her hips as she walked toward the water.

She felt free within herself, even bare, even so exposed.

That, more than anything, was a miracle.

"You do not have to wear anything at all," Erevos said from behind her, his voice low and smooth as he moved toward her, the sound of water already responding to his presence.

At that, she smiled widely. Did he know he was flirting with her?

"Would you prefer that I never wear anything at all?" she asked, turning her head just enough to look at him over her shoulder before taking his hand, her fingers curling between his, and slowly stepping into the warm, waiting water.

It welcomed her at once, silk-smooth and steaming, sliding along her ankles, her calves, and her thighs. She exhaled as it rose higher, enveloping her sore muscles, easing the tender ache between her legs.

How divine it felt to sink into that heated embrace after everything they had done. Her body was sore in every possible place—her thighs, her hips, her lower lips—and all she wanted was to soak until her fingers wrinkled and her mind went blissfully blank, to lean back against her Erevos and let him hold her there.

Her Erevos. Who was now her husband.

Perhaps not in the traditional human way, without temple leaders or vows or witnesses, but husband through and through.

Erevos moved through the inky water toward her, the dark liquid parting around his powerful body as though eager to please him. The pond was not deep—it reached just below her breasts—and she was grateful that she was tall enough not to feel swallowed by it.

She looked up at him and smiled, the steam dampening her lashes.

At once, Erevos returned his own version of a smile, the baring of sharp teeth that once terrified her.

Now she found it adorable and very much kissable.

He gathered a pool of the inky water into his hands, the liquid seeming thicker in his palms, and slowly poured it over her shoulder. The heat cascaded down her skin, sliding over her collarbone, between her breasts, and she could not help the soft sound that escaped her.

"What is that?" he asked as he gathered more water and let it spill over her other shoulder.

"What is what?" she murmured, eyes half-lidded as the warmth soaked deeper into her muscles.

"That sound," he clarified. "You made it when we mated."

Another thing she liked so much about Erevos was his curiosity, the way he studied her as though she were the most fascinating creature in existence, worthy of observation and understanding. It felt selfish to enjoy that attention so thoroughly, to bask in it as though it were sunlight, but she could not help herself. Besides, she enjoyed teaching him what she knew, even when her knowledge was laughably small compared to the vast, ancient one he had.

In her village, Lyssena had never been allowed to correct anyone. Certainly not to teach someone older than herself.

When her father misspoke, she swallowed the correction. When her brothers misbehaved, she had endured it in silence because a man knew better, because a woman's place was beneath and behind.

Standing there now, naked in a demon's bathing chamber,

explaining pleasure to a being older than realms, she realized how absurd it all was.

It had been a towering pile of boar shit.

"It is called a moan," she said, taking his hand into hers, their fingers tangling as warmth swirled around them. "It is a sound of pleasure. Sometimes the body makes it when the feeling is too much to contain."

"I have never moaned," Erevos replied, studying their joined hands. "Yet I have felt pleasure."

She smiled. "You do not make many noises at all," she teased. "Oh, but you growl."

Humans hummed and clicked their tongues, screamed and wailed, laughed loudly, and wept louder still. They were creatures of sound and expression.

Erevos, on the other hand, spoke . . . and he growled.

"I never growled before meeting you," he said.

Lyssena hummed thoughtfully at that. Perhaps she wasn't the only one changing.

She found that she enjoyed learning Erevos. Not merely his body, though she certainly enjoyed that as well, but the subtleties of him, the strange, unexpected moments that made something ancient and otherworldly feel almost . . . human.

She would never forget the way he had lounged across the princess's bed, long limbs sprawled in a posture so scandalous it would have sent half her village into hysterics, entirely oblivious to how indecent he appeared.

The memory tugged a smile from her lips, there in the steaming water. But her smile faded as she realized she had asked him so little about himself.

Since arriving in his realm, she had spoken of her village, her fears, her aches, her customs, her body, and he had listened, endlessly patient, endlessly curious, as though every small detail she offered was a treasure worth studying.

Yet she had rarely turned that same curiosity toward him.

She had made everything about herself.

The thought pricked at her chest. There, with steam curling around her shoulders and Erevos's large hand still entwined with hers, Lyssena decided that she wanted to do something for him.

He had built her a home from shadow and will, and had warmed water for her without being asked.

Oh, she loved planning things.

The realization sent a spark of excitement dancing through her, warming her more than the bath ever could. She had always been the one to imagine festivals larger than the harvest warranted, to suggest ribbons where none were necessary, to arrange flowers simply because they were beautiful. Her mother used to sigh at her dramatics.

But here? Here, there was no one to tell her she was too much.

She could plan anything from a small, intimate banquet lit by floating orbs to an entire day devoted to the two of them, filled with whatever delights she could devise. She could decorate the main hall with fabrics in deep jewel tones, drape garlands along the darkened walls, scatter cushions across the floor so he might recline as he pleased. Perhaps she could even craft something by hand. A garment, a token, something beautiful that would belong solely to him.

Oh, there was so much she could do.

Her mind whirled with possibilities, images layering over one another in a rainbow of black and imagination.

Although . . . She did not know where the shops were in this place. In fact, she did not know if there were shops at all.

She had not seen taverns, nor merchants, nor market stalls brimming with fabric and fruit and chatter. This realm did not echo with bargaining voices or clinking mugs.

Did gods even require such things?

She glanced at Erevos through the drifting steam, studying the broad line of his shoulders, the shadows that curled toward him.

She knew he never ate. Because . . . well, he was a god.

And why would gods eat?

Perhaps demons did, but she had never seen him consume anything. Not fruit, not water, not even a bite of bread or meat. As far as she knew, he simply existed.

"Tell me," she said, swaying their joined hands left and right above the surface of the water, watching the dark liquid ripple around their fingers. "Is there a place . . . to buy things here?"

"There is," he replied, drawing Lyssena closer until her body was flush against his. "There is a market in The Void."

The sentence alone sent a thrill down her spine.

Looking up at him now, she found herself pressed fully against his torso, her breasts brushing the firm plane of him, the heat of his body radiating through the thin barrier of water. The waves around them responded to his movement, rising and curling.

"And . . . " she continued as she traced the tip of her finger over the defined lines of his abdomen, following the ridges of muscle. "How did you pay when you went there last time?"

His shadows stirred at her touch.

Chapter Thirty-Six

Bubbles of Betrayal

Lyssena

Lyssena did not wake all at once, but rather surfaced slowly from sleep, her consciousness rising through warmth and soreness and the weight of strong hands on her hips, until she became aware of the dip of the mattress beneath Erevos's weight.

She kept her eyes closed.

Not because she was still asleep, though exhaustion did cling to her bones, but rather because curiosity had rooted itself in her mind, and she refused to let it go.

Erevos believed she needed rest. He had stroked her hair until her breathing evened, and had remained beside her long after her limbs had grown slack against his. He would not leave until she slept.

Or so he thought.

Through lowered lashes, she sensed the moment he finally moved. She fought the urge to peek, to watch how a god prepared to step between realms, to see whether he dissolved into smoke or tore open the air itself, but she knew that if she so much as twitched, he would notice, and she was determined to discover his secrets on her own terms.

Only when the chamber settled into a deeper silence, when the warmth beside her faded enough that the cool air brushed along her exposed shoulder, did she allow her eyes to open.

She stretched, arching her back as her arms reached above her head, and a soft sound escaped her throat at the pull between her legs, at the ache that bloomed along her hips. She was tired, undeniably so, her body spent in a way that begged for another hour beneath the covers, but beneath that fatigue she felt the thrill of planning something he did not expect.

If he went to the market alone, then she would follow.

If he would guard his mysteries, then she would uncover them, cleverly, with a smile.

With a determined exhale, Lyssena pushed aside the shadow-woven blankets and rose from the bed, unconcerned with her nakedness as the air slid over her skin and tightened her nipples, as warmth still clung to the insides of her thighs. There was something intoxicating about moving freely through this home without cloth to bind or restrict her, about feeling entirely unhidden in a place where no eyes judged and no voices whispered that a woman must cover herself for decency's sake.

The floor welcomed her bare feet, and she crossed the chamber toward the wardrobe Erevos had shaped for her, its doors rippling ever so slightly beneath her touch before parting to reveal rows upon rows of gowns spun from shadow and shimmer.

She paused there, admiring them as one might admire a gallery of treasures.

Fabrics in deep midnight blacks and wine-dark blacks cascaded beside softer blacks that glowed like moonlit smoke.

Lyssena always thought she loved the day, but she turned out to love the night more. At that, she smiled.

She trailed her fingertips along the garments, delighting in the way they responded, the material cool at first and then warming beneath her skin, sliding over her knuckles like living silk.

If she intended to step beyond this home—to venture into The Void's market—she would need her suit and her mask, the structured layers that concealed her shape and rendered her something less recognizably human, something that could walk unnoticed beside a god. The thought made her lips curve again; there was a thrill in disguise, in stepping into a role that allowed her to observe without being observed.

Still, beneath that suit . . .

Her gaze lowered slowly over her own body, and amusement flickered in her eyes.

It was undeniably delightful not to wear undergarments.

She selected a gown at last, one darker than spilled ink yet threaded with faint iridescence that shimmered when it caught the drifting light, and lifted it over her head, letting it spill down along her shoulders and breasts, over her waist and hips, the fabric settling against her skin with nothing beneath it to dull the sensation.

"How wonderfully improper," she whispered to herself, smoothing the material over her thighs, relishing the freedom of it, the absence of tight bands and laces and stiff linen that once pressed into her skin from dawn until dusk.

She adjusted the gown, and while she did, she noticed . . . White.

Not shimmering, not alive with shadow, but plain and soft and very human. Her village dress.

The ivory fabric looked simple against the richness of the surrounding gowns; its modest neckline and sleeves reminded her of another life, another version of herself who had once believed that such a dress was the height of beauty.

"This dress was probably bought with the money Father got for my life," she said, and the bitterness in her voice was so thick she could almost taste it.

The gown slipped from her grasp and swayed where it hung, innocent and pale against the living dark, and Lyssena stepped back as though it had accused her of something unspeakable.

With those dreadful thoughts clawing through her mind, she turned away from the wardrobe and made her way down the corridor toward the very first room she had occupied upon arriving in this realm, the room she had reshaped in defiance, molding it into something protective.

It no longer looked like the original space Erevos had offered her, nor did it truly resemble the one from her village; instead, it had become a fortress of memory and defense, constructed from equal parts longing and fury.

When she walked inside, the air felt still and untouched, exactly as she had left it.

"I was raised in that room at home, from the very first day of my life . . . " she murmured as she crossed the space and approached the small wooden chair that was a bat.

"And my parents kept it only for me," she continued, "even though I have brothers who share one room that was actually smaller than mine . . . "

She crouched and lifted the bat into her hands. It was cool on her palms, and for a moment, she simply stared at it.

Lyssena asked it to become a few small plates as tears pricked her eyes.

The plates clinked as her grip tightened.

"This could only mean . . . " she breathed, "This could only mean that my sole existence was for them to sell me."

A tear slid from her chin and struck the smooth surface of one plate.

"My whole purpose was to be sold."

The room did not argue with her.

It did not soften the truth or wrap it in kinder interpretations.

It simply held her there, witnessing the moment a daughter understood that love that taught you how to be alone was not the kind that taught you how to be safe.

Well, that was easy, Lyssena thought to herself as she walked out of the mouth of the cave, the stone arch curving above her like the lip of some great slumbering beast that neither questioned nor stopped her departure.

Being alone in The Void started to feel a little wrong. Especially without Erevos.

The vastness stretched before her exactly as it always had. It was endless and dark, with a sky that did not look like a sky at all. Nothing appeared different since the last time she went outside; the shadows drifted as they pleased, the distant horizon blurred into obscurity, and the ground beneath her feet remained smooth and unmoving at all.

Perhaps it had not. Perhaps she was overthinking everything.

With the mask secured over her face, the suit sealed neatly along her body, and a small pile of tear bubbles made of shadow cradled carefully in her hands, Lyssena continued forward. She felt smart and resourceful.

Very proud of herself.

Creating those small tea plates and filling them with her

tears had been a very clever idea. She had watched the droplets gather and tremble before sealing them inside the shadow-formed porcelain, had felt the slight tremor in her fingers as she asked the plates to close, and of course, they had obeyed, folding inward.

That was indeed very resourceful.

Erevos had explained that the currency in The Void was emotion; it was so matter-of-fact in his tone as though such a system were entirely ordinary. Lyssena had not understood, at first, how one could physically hold an emotion, how something so intangible and internal could be offered across a counter like bread or fabric, until she realized that some emotions burned behind the eyes or tightened the throat.

Some left proof.

She still had no clue why gods or demons needed those emotions, what use ancient beings had for something as fragile and fleeting as sorrow or joy, but she was also far too impatient to wait for answers.

For now, she had somewhere to be.

Lyssena wanted to go to the market, and she did exactly that.

Chapter Thirty-Seven

Under the Sun

Erevos

The market was full of humans.

Erevos enjoyed feeding on emotions—the tang of envy, the warm bloom of joy, the metallic pulse of fear, and the sweetness of devotion—but noise was an entirely different matter.

Emotion was sustenance.

Noise was intrusion.

Voices overlapped, merchants calling out prices, children shrieking as they darted between stalls, livestock bleating in protest as rough hands tugged at rope halters. Wooden wheels creaked over uneven stone, iron-shod hooves struck the ground in impatient rhythms, and somewhere nearby a human laughed too loudly, the sound cracking through the air like splintering timber.

One of the things he preferred was quiet.

True quiet, the kind that existed in The Void, where silence did not mean absence but depth, where stillness was thick and intentional and undisturbed by meaningless chatter. In the human world, quiet existed only in the hour before dawn, in the breath held between confessions, in the pause before a blade struck.

Unfortunately for Erevos, it was midday.

The sun stood high above the village square, its light glaring against thatched rooftops and whitewashed stone. Stalls lined the open space in crooked rows, canvas awnings sagging slightly beneath the weight of daylight, bolts of dyed fabric swaying beside strings of drying herbs and garlands of garlic.

A butcher's table stood not far from the well, slabs of red meat glistening wetly as flies gathered in spirals, while beside it a fishmonger shouted over the din, holding up silver bodies that caught the sun like flashing blades.

Humans brushed against one another without thought or apology, fabric scraping fabric, shoulders knocking, coins clinking as they exchanged hands slick with labor. Irritation at haggled prices, pride at a good bargain, hunger, impatience, fleeting attraction, and suspicion.

It was abundant.

It was chaotic and loud.

I shall obtain a soothing salve, he thought as he slipped from one shadow into the next, his form dissolving and reforming along the narrow seams where light failed to reach. But where would he find such a thing? In truth, he wished to obtain many, enough that his songbird would never lack even the smallest comfort, enough that she would never again feel tenderness without remedy waiting at his hand.

He should have asked her.

Patience, he reminded himself.

From one stall to the next, Erevos searched without being seen, drifting through shade cast by awnings and carts, listening to the clipped exchanges between merchants and customers, studying jars of dried herbs, bundles of roots, and small clay pots sealed with wax. He found tinctures for coughs, salves for burns, powders meant to steady trembling hands, yet none bore any clear indication that they would soothe the particular ache he sought to ease.

An idea rose in his mind. If he followed the scent of mating, surely he would find the medicine associated with it.

Where humans coupled, there would be remedies.

So he turned his attention from sight to smell, from noise to the subtler currents beneath it, and allowed himself to sift through the air thick with sweat and livestock and fermenting grain until he located the scent of arousal.

He moved beyond the market stalls toward the homes that loomed over them, their upper stories, and he listened carefully for the rhythm of flesh striking flesh, for the uneven breaths and the strained, wavering sounds Lyssena called "moaning".

The scent drew him toward a building he recognized as a tavern, a place where humans consumed bitter liquids in alarming quantities and grew progressively louder with each cup emptied. Of course, what he sought would be found in the loudest place.

With little choice and even less patience remaining, Erevos slid through the shadow beneath a merchant's cart and emerged within the dim rear corridor of the largest tavern in the village, the air inside heavy with ale, smoke, and the dense, humid tang of bodies packed too closely together.

As he advanced down the narrow hall, the sounds intensified—low groans and the wet cadence of movement—and the scent of arousal thickened until it coated the back of his throat.

There, behind a closed door barely latched, were two humans.

The female knelt bare upon the floorboards, her knees pressed into worn wood, one hand wrapped around the cock of a wrinkled male whose face bore thick, uneven patches of hair. Her spine curved forward as she leaned toward him, her lips parting as she guided him into her mouth.

"Mhm . . . what a thick cock you have, master," the woman whispered before sliding that same cock past her lips.

Erevos stilled.

First, he had now observed what a human cock looked like, and it was far from thick at all. Second, that particular cock would have never caused the need for a salve.

A slow, wide grin spread across his face, sharp teeth flashing briefly in the dimness, amusement curling through him.

Humans exaggerated.

Humans lied even during mating.

Still, he had come for a purpose.

Dissolving into shadow once more, Erevos slipped beneath the bed and then into the adjoining rooms, searching along shelves and inside chests, examining small jars and folded cloths for any indication of a soothing balm.

He found none.

Erevos searched longer than he intended, drifting from chamber to chamber, from cupboard to crate, examining clay pots and folded linens with growing dissatisfaction, yet nowhere did he find the salve he sought, nowhere a jar clearly marked for the soothing of tender flesh. He had been gone too long.

His songbird was alone.

He withdrew from yet another tavern's stale corridors and returned to the open air, allowing the sunlit chaos of the village to wash over him once more as he considered a more efficient approach.

If mating did not lead him to the salve, perhaps mother-hood would.

He turned his attention toward the quieter edges of the market, where homes stood closer together, and the noise softened into domestic murmurs, the scrape of chairs, the murmur of lullabies, the whispers of a child being rocked.

It did not take him long to find her.

A woman stood just outside a modest dwelling, her skirts plain and her hair loosely bound, laughing as a small child clung to her leg.

Erevos watched from the shade of a nearby wall as she lifted the child into her arms and carried it inside, her voice lowering into gentle tones meant to coax sleep. He waited, listening to the gradual quieting of the child's restless movements, to the soft cadence of breath evening out behind thin wooden walls.

Only when the house settled into true silence did he move.

Erevos no longer bothered to hide himself. He stepped from the shadow directly into her small chamber.

The woman turned at once. Her eyes widened so violently that the whites showed stark against her irises, her breath catching in a sharp, strangled sound as terror flooded her features. The scent of fear bloomed thick, prickling along Erevos's senses as her entire body began to tremble.

She dropped to her knees just like his songbird did when she first saw him.

Her palms struck the floorboards, her head bowing so quickly that her hair fell forward to shield her face, and she averted her gaze as though even the act of looking upon him might condemn her.

"G-Greatest god," she stammered, her voice shaking so hard the words nearly fractured, "forgive me—"

Erevos stood there, tall and unmoving, his presence filling the small room. He did not have time for all these human customs. His Lyssena was hurting, and he was losing time.

"I require a salve," he said, his tone neither cruel nor kind. "One used after mating."

Her trembling intensified.

For a fleeting moment, shame flickered through her fear, coloring it with mortification, but she did not dare question him. With shaking hands, she rose just enough to crawl toward a low shelf near the bed, her fingers fumbling among small jars and cloth-wrapped bundles before retrieving a modest clay container sealed with wax.

She held it out to him without lifting her gaze.

"This . . . this is what we use, Greatest," she whispered, her voice barely more than breath. "For soreness. For . . . for comfort."

Erevos stepped closer, and she flinched despite herself, her shoulders curling inward as though bracing for impact.

He took the jar between his fingers and examined it, turning it, noting the scent of herbs and oil.

"This is the correct substance?" he asked.

"Yes, Greatest god," she answered at once.

"Where may I obtain more of it?"

The question seemed to surprise her more than his presence had.

Silence stretched thin before she swallowed hard and pressed her forehead fully to the floor.

"My humble self would make it for you," she said. "If it pleases you, I would prepare as much as you require."

Erevos should have started with it. He could have had the salve and the knowledge.

"Teach me," he said at last.

Her breath hitched.

Slowly, cautiously, she nodded against the floorboards, her entire body still trembling as she whispered, "Yes, Greatest god."

Chapter Thirty-Eight

The Guide With Two Tails

Lyssena

"What a cute cat!" Lyssena exclaimed with so much joy that she immediately forgot she was meant to be quiet, her voice carrying farther into The Void than she would have preferred.

She froze for a heartbeat after the words left her mouth, suddenly aware of how alone she was.

Being alone in The Void was a danger in itself, even if nothing had yet happened from the shifting horizon to threaten her, even if she had walked for quite some time without encountering a single other being. The landscape had remained vast and strangely still, shadows drifting lazily along the ground as though indifferent to her presence.

Until this cat.

Well . . . it was not exactly the sort of cat she had known in her village, not the small barn creatures that hunted mice and tolerated affection on their own temperamental terms, but it looked close enough that her heart had reacted before her mind could intervene.

It had the shape of a cat, with a lithe body and those fuzzy little toe beans she adored so much. It was just . . . slightly unusual.

This cat had the same eyes as Erevos—deep, endless, and purple—and far too many sharp teeth visible even when its mouth was closed. It also had two tails.

And two sets of eyes.

And, upon closer inspection, it seemed to possess two of everything, layered over itself as though one creature had been folded imperfectly atop another.

"You . . . look very . . . interesting," Lyssena murmured as she lowered herself to sit, leaning back on her heels, her masked gaze studying the creature with fascination rather than fear.

Up until she had met this peculiar feline, she had been feeling the weight of her journey settle into her limbs, her calves, and her shoulders, burned from walking so long through terrain that never seemed to change. Her fingers, too, ached from cradling the tear bubbles she had so cleverly created, the small spheres of shadow sealed around her sorrow.

Holding them constantly was becoming inconvenient. Resourceful as ever, Lyssena had asked the suit for pockets.

The suit, at first, had not responded. That silence had made Lyssena a little nervous, a brief tightening in her chest as she wondered whether she had overestimated her authority over the living fabric wrapped around her body. However, after a few moments of thoughtful explanation—after describing in great detail what pockets were, how they functioned, and why they were useful—she felt the material shift against her hips.

Seams formed and openings appeared. Pockets.

Lyssena had been delighted beyond measure.

Carefully, she had tucked the tear bubbles away, relieved

not only by the freedom of her hands but also by the discretion it offered. She had no intention of arriving at the market displaying all the currency she possessed, not when she did not yet understand the rules of this place. What if someone attempted to steal from her? What if some creature sensed the grief sealed within those spheres and decided it wanted it for itself?

What if this, and what if that? No.

That simply would not happen when Lyssena was managing everything so remarkably well on her own.

Now, sitting before the strange two-tailed creature, she tilted her head and decided to speak.

"Are you hungry?" she asked, genuinely curious, and silently hoping that Void cats did not, in fact, consume wandering women.

The cat tilted its head to the side in a mirrored motion, its multiple eyes blinking slowly, and Lyssena chose to interpret that as a no.

At that, she tilted her head further. "Can you understand me?"

The cat merely stared at her for a long moment before lowering itself gracefully onto the dark ground and rolling to expose its belly, both tails flicking lazily behind it.

"Oh, aren't you a sweetheart!" Lyssena exclaimed as she leaned forward to scratch at the offered belly through the barrier of her gloved fingers. "So much soft fur . . . oh, I wish I could remove the suit and feel you with my bare hands."

The creature swayed from side to side, stretching in a way that presented different angles of its plush, soft-looking underside, its many eyes half-lidded in what appeared to be bliss.

Lyssena laughed beneath her mask.

"Perhaps you know where the market is," she ventured,

smoothing her fingers along its fur. "If you do, could you show me the way?"

It might have been considered strange—asking directions from a random, double-eyed, double-tailed Void cat—but very little in this shadowed world operated according to the rules she once understood, and so far, curiosity had rewarded her far more often than fear.

So she decided to trust it.

After a long moment, the cat rolled back onto all fours, its tails curling upward like twin question marks before settling behind it, and without so much as a backward glance, it began to walk.

The cat led Lyssena in a very specific direction, its twin tails swaying in slow, synchronized arcs. She was not entirely certain whether this was the way to the market or somewhere else entirely, but the creature was so very confident that she found she could not bring herself to doubt it.

Whenever she paused, the cat would stop as well, turning to fix its many violet eyes upon her. It was unmistakable. It *wanted* her to follow.

And so, she did.

Together, Lyssena and her strange new companion passed beneath dense trees the color of crushed, overripe pomegranate, a deep, almost blackened crimson that seemed to drink in what little ambient light existed in The Void. Not a single leaf stirred overhead. Not one. The canopy remained perfectly still, suspended in an unnatural pause, as though time itself had forgotten to move through this place.

Lyssena thought that if she were ever able to walk these lands without her mask or suit, her hair would never whip into her eyes, never cling to her lips, never tangle at the nape of her neck with sweat. She liked that very much.

It was so quiet here.

Lyssena had always believed she preferred loud places, like the overlapping chatter of neighbors, the shrieks of children racing through narrow streets, the constant noise of a home too full to ever feel empty. That was what she had known, after all, with five brothers and endless afternoons spent helping her mother's friends rock crying infants or chase mischievous toddlers from one room to the next. Noise had meant life. Noise had meant belonging.

And yet here, in this vast and muted expanse where even her own footsteps seemed softened against the ground, she felt . . . content.

She imagined her babies walking through this quiet place. They would likely wear masks at first, until they grew strong and divine like Erevos; until they, too, became little gods of The Void. The thought filled her chest with a warmth so bright it nearly ached.

Oh, Lyssena truly wished for a small family here in the quiet heart of this endless dark.

As the cat suddenly stopped and turned left, its tails curling upward, she noticed the mouth of a cave set into a low rise of stone. It was far smaller than the cavern where she and Erevos had made their home, its entrance narrow, with no rivers weaving black paths nearby.

She found herself thinking, not for the first time, of how wisely Erevos had chosen their dwelling, how instinctively he had selected a place both grand and hidden, powerful yet private. Pride swelled in her chest at the thought of him. Her husband.

Lyssena enjoyed beyond reason calling him that, savoring the word as though it were a secret sweetness meant only for her. Husband. It was what she had always wanted, a family of her own, children to cradle and guide, to show such overwhelming kindness and love that they would never, not for a single breath of their existence, feel alone.

"Do you want me to go inside that cave?" she asked, tilting her head at the cat.

But instead of entering, the creature turned on its paws and began walking in a different direction, not sparing the cave another glance.

Without hesitation, Lyssena followed.

And when the trees began to thin, and the stillness changed, she understood.

That was the market.

Chapter Thirty-Nine

Erevos's Human

Lyssena

Lyssena saw the market long before she even considered stepping out of the forest.

At first, she thought the horizon itself had fractured, that the flat, endless dark of The Void had grown jagged and uneven, but as she stepped forward and narrowed her gaze, she realized the shapes were not landscape at all.

They were structures. Black stalls rose from the shadowed ground like carved obsidian, draped in fabrics so dark they seemed to swallow what little ambient light touched them. The awnings did not flutter but hung heavy, as though sculpted rather than sewn. Tables stretched beneath them, laden with objects she could not yet distinguish from this distance.

And between those stalls—

Lyssena stopped walking.

Dozens of figures moved among them. All tall. All ink-black. All crowned with those endless purple eyes.

Her breath caught somewhere between her lungs and her throat.

They were like Erevos.

Not identical, no, not quite, but surely of the same origin. Some stood with backs that sagged unnaturally forward, their elongated arms nearly brushing the ground as they drifted rather than walked. Others appeared fluid, their limbs tapering and reforming as though shaped from thick ink, edges blurring and pulling back into themselves with each slow step. One figure's silhouette bristled with long, tapering spikes that rose from its shoulders and spine like thorns carved from night itself, while another looked too soft, rounder in shape, its form plush and heavy, like some enormous shadow-made beast draped in velvet darkness.

Yet all of them towered.

They moved, gliding between stalls, leaning toward one another, their bodies folding and unfolding in ways that made Lyssena's human mind struggle to follow their anatomy.

She had not expected this. Not this scale.

Not this . . . multitude.

Her fingers curled slowly against the fabric of her suit as she swallowed hard, the sound loud in her own ears despite the distance that still separated her from them. A faint, unfamiliar tightness began to wind itself around her ribs.

This was Erevos's world.

And she was suddenly aware of how small she was within it.

Excitement fluttered first because this was what she had wanted, wasn't it? To see more, to understand more, to step beyond the cavern and into the vastness he belonged to.

But that excitement soured quickly . . . What had she been thinking?

The market did not resemble the lively human squares she knew, filled with fabric and laughter and the scent of bread. This place felt immense and ancient and powerful. The ground itself seemed thicker here, the shadows pooling more densely between the stalls, as though they were drawn toward the gathered divinity like moths to flame.

Lyssena's pulse began to quicken. If any one of them wished her harm—

Her stomach dropped. She would not be able to shield herself.

Her suit was clever; it listened and adapted, but she was not Erevos. She did not dissolve into darkness. She did not tower.

She was a woman wrapped in borrowed protection, standing at the edge of a gathering of gods.

Her throat tightened.

For a fleeting, treacherous moment, she regretted leaving home at all. Regretted her confidence. Regretted believing that curiosity alone would carry her safely through a realm she did not yet understand.

She forced herself to inhale. She drew it in slowly through her nose, then let it out just as carefully, steadying the tremor threatening to take root in her hands.

Breathe.

She could not turn back now. Not when she had come this far.

Lyssena lifted her chin and tried very hard to appear as though her heart was not beating like something desperate to escape her chest.

From afar, the market of gods watched no one in particular. And yet she felt as though it already saw her.

"Do you think they will eat me?" she whispered to the cat,

who wove lazily between her legs, its twin tails brushing against her calves like soft, living ribbons of shadow.

"Probably not."

The voice was deep, smooth, and threaded with something darkly amused, and it did not belong to her.

Lyssena nearly screamed, the sound climbing upward from her chest before she strangled it down into silence, her entire body going rigid as goosebumps rippled violently beneath the living fabric of her suit, the fine hairs along her arms and the nape of her neck prickling.

Who said that?

It had not been the cat—of that she was entirely certain—and yet the voice had sounded close, as though it had been spoken directly into the hollow space just behind her ear.

Her gaze darted to the left, and then to the right, where the market stretched in endless ink-dark rows, but she saw no one standing near enough to have addressed her.

Then she heard a single step behind her.

She turned quickly, heart hammering so violently she felt it in her ears, only to find nothing there at all, nothing but open space and the dense, unmoving shadows of The Void.

"I am Rolam. Nice to meet you, human."

Lyssena spun back around so fast the motion made her slightly dizzy, and this time the scream did not even manage to form because she forgot how to breathe altogether.

A god stood directly before her.

He had not approached—she would have seen him—and yet there he was, towering and way too close.

She stumbled backward without thinking, one step and then another as her pulse roared in her ears.

And still, the cat purred.

A low, vibrating sound rolled through the space between them as the creature pressed itself affectionately against the god's leg, carding along him, as though greeting something known and entirely safe.

This demon-god almost looked like Erevos. The same ink-black height, the same endless violet eyes that appeared to stare through rather than at her, the same sculpted darkness that gave the impression of a body formed from concentrated night.

Even the air around him felt colder, and she could not shake the unnerving sensation that he had not walked toward her at all, but had simply decided to exist in that exact space.

Though one thing distinguished this one from her own god, at that was the big, gray scar all over his chest.

Lyssena realized she was staring. Her gaze dropped instinctively as she suddenly remembered all of the rules that took over her life.

"Even when you're not in the village, you will not meet my gaze?" Rolam asked, his voice smooth and playful, as though he found her reluctance more amusing than offensive.

"How . . . how can I . . . ?" Lyssena's entire body trembled, as every lesson she had ever learned about reverence and divinity came rushing back into her mind all at once. "You are a god—"

At that, Rolam laughed, and the sound startled her more than his sudden appearance had, because it was very human in its cadence, a laugh that might have belonged in a tavern or around a dinner table, not echoing from the chest of a giant ink-black being born of The Void.

"There are no gods, silly little human," he replied. "We are demons, creatures of The Void. Nothing more, and certainly nothing like your kind invented."

Lyssena could not dispel the dissonance curling through her thoughts, because everything about him felt wrong in a way she could not properly articulate. Not wrong in the sense of danger, though danger was certainly there, but wrong in the way his voice carried such familiar inflection, such conversational ease, as though he had spent far too long listening to human speech and had learned to wear it comfortably.

"Come now," he continued, tilting his head ever so slightly. "Leave those foolish rules behind. Tell me, do you like honey and cinnamon?"

The question struck her with such absurd normalcy that for a moment she simply stared at him. Why would he ask her that?

What possible place did honey and cinnamon have in a market of shadowed demons?

Her throat felt dry as she swallowed, and slowly she lifted her gaze to meet his, forcing herself to endure the intensity of those endless violet eyes that did not blink.

He did not sound overtly threatening, and yet there was something about him she could not quite name. Something too observant, too aware.

"I do," she answered at last, her voice soft but steady despite the frantic pulse still fluttering beneath her ribs, and she barely had time to wonder what explanation could possibly follow such an oddly domestic question—

"So you are Erevos's human," Rolam said. "He came to me and purchased honey and spices."

Lyssena blinked.

The market, the towering forms, the awareness of being surrounded by creatures far older and more powerful than herself—all of it seemed to shift slightly out of focus as her mind struggled to reconcile this new information.

A strange warmth unfurled in her chest despite herself, softening the tense line of her shoulders, and for reasons she could not fully explain, she felt more at ease than she had only moments before.

This demon—this Rolam—sold human food.

Why?

For what purpose would beings of The Void require honey or spice, substances born of sunlit fields and mortal kitchens?

She did not know.

And somehow, that unanswered question unsettled her far more deeply than his laughter had.

Chapter Forty

Three Bubbles and a Truth

Lyssena

Lyssena walked beside Rolam, careful to keep a respectful distance between them, though not so much that it would appear rude, her hands resting lightly at her sides as she tried to steady the fluttering unease in her chest.

She did not fully understand why she had chosen to trust him.

Perhaps it was the way he spoke—not like the others who moved in near silence between the stalls, but with an ease that resembled human conversation. Perhaps it was the laughter he had offered her earlier, so startlingly familiar that it had disrupted her fear. Or perhaps it was simply that she had already stepped too far into this world to retreat now, and trust, however fragile, was easier than admitting how vulnerable she truly was.

They walked between the towering dark stalls of The Void

market, where all the other demons seemed to pay no attention to them at all.

"Did Erevos give you the tear-bubbles," Rolam asked so casually, as though inquiring about the weather, "or did you create them yourself?"

Lyssena's breath caught. Her hand moved instinctively toward her hip, toward the pocket where the small spheres rested securely against her thigh, and she looked up at him in open surprise.

"How did you know what I carry?" she asked.

Rolam's mouth curved. "You are walking through a market of demons," he replied. "You think we cannot sense grief when it brushes against us?"

Lyssena swallowed, "I made them," she admitted quietly. "I wished to buy something for Erevos . . . for our home."

At that, Rolam's gaze shifted slightly, studying her. "And what were you thinking of purchasing?"

She hesitated, because now that she stood here, surrounded by towering beings of shadow exchanging objects she barely understood, her ideas felt embarrassingly small.

As they continued walking, Lyssena allowed her gaze to drift across the stalls, trying to gather some understanding of what this market offered. There were not many demons present—perhaps ten or a few more in total—they were positioned far away from one another. The demons exchanged small containers and narrow boxes, all crafted from condensed shadow.

The exchanges were nearly silent.

No loud bargaining, no raised voices, no laughter echoing across the square. Only the faintest murmur now and then.

She noticed that the containers varied in shape, some tall and slender like sealed vials, others broad and square, their surfaces matte and lightless, and though she could not see inside them, she felt certain that whatever they held was not physical in the way honey and cinnamon were.

The realization made her feel even more conspicuous. What could she possibly offer in a place like this?

As if sensing her growing unease, the two-tailed creature slipped between her and Rolam once more, its soft body brushing against her ankle before gliding toward his side.

Lyssena looked down at it, then up at Rolam.

"Is this your cat?" she asked.

Rolam's grin widened, and for a moment it resembled Erevos's own, though not quite as expansive, not quite as sharp, but similar enough to make her chest tighten.

"This," he said, glancing down at the creature as it circled his leg, "is not a cat as you understand them in the human realm. It is a herta."

"A herta," Lyssena repeated, testing the unfamiliar word on her tongue. "Does the herta have a name?"

"No," Rolam replied without hesitation.

She blinked at him. "Why not?"

As she asked the question, her gaze drifted once more across the market, and it was then that she noticed that there were no decorations.

No fabrics meant purely for beauty, no carvings, no trinkets or ornaments designed to delight the eye. Every stall held containers, sealed vessels, shadow-bound items, but nothing frivolous, nothing crafted solely for admiration.

No color beyond black and violet. No excess.

And suddenly the idea of buying something "nice" for their home felt impossibly human.

"You are disappointed," Rolam said.

Lyssena hesitated because denying it would have been pointless, and there was something strangely exhausting about pretending in a place where even sealed grief could be sensed through fabric and shadow.

"There is . . . nothing for me to buy," she admitted at last, her gaze drifting once more over the dark stalls and their purposeful wares. "I thought there might be cushions, perhaps, or plush pillows, or something soft to place near our seating area. Or decorations. Or—" she faltered, realizing how trivial her ideas must sound here, "—anything, really."

She could almost see the image in her mind: a corner of their cavern softened with fabric, something inviting and warm against the endless dark stone, a space that felt less like a realm of ancient power and more like a home.

Rolam regarded her in silence for a moment before replying, "Demons do not sell such things."

The statement was simple. And for the first time since he had begun speaking to her, he did not sound particularly human.

A human, she thought, would have elaborated. A human would have added something, an explanation, a suggestion, perhaps even a shrug and a redirection toward some other stall or merchant who might offer what she sought. A human conversation filled the spaces between answers.

Rolam left the space empty.

Just like he did not answer her question about naming the herta.

It was not cruel, nor dismissive, but final in a way that felt distinctly inhuman, as though the matter required no further examination because, to him, it simply did not exist.

Lyssena pressed her lips together, unwilling to surrender her idea so easily. She also wanted to scratch her nose, but then remembered she had a beak.

Well, if such things were not displayed here, that did not necessarily mean they were not available at all.

"Then, do you sell such things?" she ventured, lifting her gaze to him once more. "You said you sold Erevos honey and spices, which are not of The Void, so I could assume you might sell other goods as well?"

She had almost said *human goods*.

The phrase hovered dangerously close to her tongue, but something about it unsettled her. She was not trembling as before, and she was not consumed by fear, but she was also not foolish enough to forget where she stood.

Rolam studied her for a long moment; those endless violet eyes were unreadable, and then he inclined his head in a slow nod.

"I do," he said simply.

The herta brushed once more against his leg, its many eyes blinking.

"Come," Rolam added, turning, his long legs already beginning to move between the shadowed stalls. "Follow me."

And though Lyssena knew she should hesitate—knew she was placing a great deal of trust into a being she had met only moments ago—she found herself walking after him anyway.

"This is amazing!" Lyssena exclaimed as she stepped fully into the deeper cavern Rolam had led her to.

The shop was set within a smaller offshoot of the market, a cave tucked farther into the dark stone, where the shadows seemed thicker but somehow more curated, as though shaped specifically to frame what lay within. Shelves carved directly from the cavern walls stretched upward in arching rows, holding objects both familiar and unsettling. There were bolts of fabric in muted, rich tones—deep burgundy, dusky gold, soft ash-gray—their textures ranging from silken sheen to heavy, plush weave. There were glass vessels filled with preserved herbs and powders, their contents layered in gradients of color, and beside them stood tall, narrow jars containing what appeared to be dried animal organs, shriveled and darkened with age.

Small shadow-crafted boxes sat in neat arrangements across long stone tables, their lids slightly ajar to reveal glimpses of jewels, polished bones, carved trinkets, and things Lyssena could not immediately name.

Rolam had everything.

Anything she could possibly imagine, and several things she could not.

She moved forward as though pulled by an invisible rope and stopped beside a small open case lined with dark velvet, inside of which rested a collection of luminous pearls, catching the faint violet glow of the cavern in a way that made them appear even prettier.

Her mouth parted in astonishment.

"How much would something like this cost?" she asked, reaching down to lift the box.

"Three bubbles," Rolam replied, "and a truth."

Lyssena turned toward him at once, the small case cradled in her gloved hands.

He was leaning casually against a broad stone table behind him, the surface beside him strewn with folded fabrics and several tall glasses containing those same dried organs she had noticed earlier.

They were unsettling. But the pearls . . . The pearls were exquisite.

"What truth?" she asked, already reaching into her pocket to retrieve three of the tear-bubbles.

Her mind was racing ahead of her even as she spoke. She

could sew the pearls into her crown so that they rested like soft constellations against the shadowed metal, or stitch them along the neckline of her gown, letting them catch the dim glow of the cavern when she moved. She could even craft two matching bracelets—one for herself and one for Erevos—something pretty and intimate that tied them together.

"Have you chosen to stay here?" Rolam asked.

The question slipped between her thoughts and stilled them entirely.

"Chosen?" she repeated.

She had chosen to follow Erevos. She had chosen to leave the human world behind. And over time, she had come to like him—more than like him, if she were honest—though the full shape of that feeling still felt too delicate to examine directly. Romance had always lived vividly in her imagination, and what she shared with Erevos had grown into something beautiful.

She was still too shy to name it fully, but she knew it was there.

And yet, Rolam's question lodged somewhere deeper than she expected.

When she had first been intimate with Erevos, she now remembered, he had said that eternity was forever.

That word had slipped past her then.

Now it had settled heavily in her mind.

"Why do you ask?" she replied at last.

Rolam's expression did not change much, but something in his gaze darkened.

"My human," he said, "never chose me back."

Chapter Forty-One

Unbearable Silence

Erevos

"Does it look correct?" Erevos asked, holding the small clay vessel between his fingers.

He was seated at the woman's rough wooden kitchen table, and the contrast between him and the modest human dwelling was almost grotesque. The ceiling beams seemed too low above him, the hearth too small, the very air too thin to contain the vastness of what he was.

Across from him, the woman stood rigid, her hands clasped so tightly before her apron that her knuckles had blanched white, her gaze fixed somewhere near his elbow rather than upon his face.

She did not dare meet his eyes.

She avoided his gaze just as Lyssena once had when they first stood before one another.

"It . . . it is perfect, Greatest," she whispered, her voice thin and strained, her entire body shaking in small tremors that made the fabric of her skirts rustle with each unsteady breath.

"Look at it," Erevos said, tilting the jar toward her. Instead of lifting her gaze, she shook harder.

"I—I trust it is as it should be," she stammered, her eyes squeezing shut altogether now, as though blindness were safer than sight.

Erevos regarded her for a long moment, observing the rigid line of her shoulders, the rapid flutter of her pulse at the base of her throat, the thick bloom of fear scenting the air around her. He had told her several times that she might look at him. He had clarified that he would not harm her. He had even softened his tone—marginally.

None of it had altered the outcome.

After a pause, he decided the effort was unnecessary.

"It will suffice," he concluded.

The woman exhaled, and Erevos rose from the table, his height forcing the kitchen into deeper shadow as his presence expanded, the corners of the room darkening in response to him like obedient hounds moving closer to their master.

"You have been efficient," he said. "Thank you."

Gratitude was a human custom.

Without further explanation, Erevos allowed his shadows to unfurl.

They slipped from beneath his feet and along the walls like living ink, pooling at the threshold before vanishing entirely into the seams of the house, into the cracks between timber and stone, into the narrow spaces where light never lingered.

The woman made a strangled sound in her throat but did not move.

Moments passed.

Then the shadows returned.

They re-entered the kitchen, coiling upward before solidifying at Erevos's side, depositing at his feet a heavy leather sack that struck the wooden floor with a heavy weight. The sound alone caused the woman to flinch violently.

Erevos bent to retrieve it and placed the bag upon the table between them. Coins shifted inside with a thick metallic clink.

The woman stared at it.

At first, she did not move. Then, slowly, cautiously, her gaze dropped to the mouth of the sack, where the drawstring had loosened just enough to reveal the gleam of gold and silver within.

Her breath left her in a broken whisper.

It was more coin than most households would see in several lifetimes.

"For the ingredients," Erevos said evenly. "And for your time."

Her knees buckled, and she caught herself against the edge of the table, eyes wide. Erevos observed her reaction with mild curiosity. Humans valued metal greatly.

It seemed appropriate compensation for the preservation of his songbird's comfort.

"You taught me how to take care of my songbird. For that I am grateful."

Without further ceremony, Erevos dissolved into shadow, leaving behind the scent of cold night and the overwhelming weight of fortune upon her kitchen table.

The cavern was wrong.

Erevos knew it the moment he emerged from shadow into the familiar vastness of their home, the shadow walls arching high above him, the slow river of darkness winding its silent path along the far edge of the chamber. Everything was exactly as it had been when he left. And yet . . . It was wrong.

"Lyssena."

He did not raise his voice because he did not need to; his voice carried regardless, threading through the cavern like a low current. No answer came.

He stepped forward, his gaze sweeping across the seating area she had begun to arrange. Her presence lingered in the air, a trace of warmth woven into the otherwise cool stillness of The Void.

But she was not there.

Erevos moved deeper into the cavern, his stride lengthening as he passed into adjoining chambers, each space carved from shadowed stone. It was all empty.

"Lyssena."

This time her name carried more weight, and with that, the shadows responded. They stirred along the walls at once, rising toward him, stretching outward in thin, searching tendrils that slipped into crevices and along ceilings, beneath stone ledges and into narrow passages where even she could not easily tread.

Find her.

The shadows dispersed, racing outward through the vast network of tunnels that laced the hill, slipping across thresholds, pouring through unseen seams in reality itself.

Erevos stood very still in the center of their home and waited. He had never needed to wait for his shadows before. But now they returned with nothing.

So he expanded his reach. The shadows thickened, flooding outward in greater volume, spreading like a tide beyond the boundaries of their cavern and into the wider expanse of The Void, brushing against distant structures, skimming across the market's outer edges, tracing the contours of familiar territories.

He could feel them straining, and yet he could not feel her.

Erevos attempted to narrow his focus, to refine the search, to isolate the distinct pattern of her presence among the countless currents of darkness.

He could sense other demons; he could sense the slow churn of traded grief and sealed emotion within shadowed containers at the market.

He could sense the hum of ancient energies shifting beneath the surface of The Void.

But Lyssena . . . He could not find her. Something unfamiliar began to unfurl within him, not irritation, nor anger. It was sharper and colder.

It felt as though a fissure had opened somewhere deep within his vast, ancient core, and from it poured something raw and destabilizing.

He had existed through centuries. He had endured the slow erosion of time that claimed even demons less careful than himself.

He had never feared.

Now the cavern felt enormous and suffocating, the silence no longer thick and intentional but oppressive, echoing back at him with unbearable emptiness.

She had been here.

She had walked these stones.

She had spoken his name in this space.

And now there was only stillness.

Erevos's form shifted, edges sharpening, shadows clinging more tightly to him as though reacting to the tremor beneath his composure. Where was she?

The question tore through him.

For the first time in his long existence, Erevos felt true fear.

If harm had come to her—

The thought did not finish.

The shadows around him began to writhe, responding to the surge of emotion he no longer bothered to suppress, the cavern darkening as his control thinned.

"Lyssena," he said again, but this time her name was not a call.

It was a plea.

And the silence that answered him was unbearable.

Chapter Forty-Two

The Option That No Longer Existed

Lyssena

The pearls felt weightless.

"My human," Rolam said, "never chose me back."

She lowered the case slowly onto the table between them, the sound of velvet against shadow sounding louder than it should have in the cavern's hush.

"You loved her?" she asked.

It felt like a fragile question, though she was not entirely sure why. Perhaps because love, when spoken by a demon, sounded less like warmth.

Rolam did not look offended by it. If anything, his expression softened.

"I did not know what it was at first," he replied. "She was . . . curious. Unafraid in ways the others were not. She would ask me questions instead of running."

Lyssena could picture a human woman standing before him, chin lifted, unaware of the vastness she was addressing.

"I returned the next season," Rolam continued, though

something quieter threaded beneath his voice. "And then the next. Eventually, I found that waiting an entire year between visits was . . . hard."

"So I came every month. Then every week."

His fingers idly traced the rim of one of the tall glass jars beside him, and Lyssena noticed another thing that was different from Erevos. Rolam acted more human.

"And then," he finished, "every day."

"You became attached," she said.

"I became obsessed," Rolam corrected without hesitation.

There was no shame in the admission.

"I learned her languages. Plural," he added. "I took her across oceans. Showed her mountains that cut into the sky. Deserts that swallowed the horizon. Cities bright enough to rival stars."

As he spoke, his voice carried more color than Lyssena had heard from anyone.

"I began to feel more," he said, then paused as though he sank deep into thought. "Impatience when she did not smile. Satisfaction when she did. Irritation at other men who approached her. Pride when she chose my company."

His gaze flicked toward Lyssena then, searching her expression.

"Demons do not experience such gradual escalation. We hunger. We take. We discard. It is efficient."

"And yet," Lyssena murmured.

"And yet," he agreed.

Lyssena became acutely aware of the steady beat of her own pulse beneath her skin.

"What happened?" she asked.

Rolam was silent for a moment. "As years passed," he said at last, "she changed."

"She aged," she whispered.

"Yes."

The single syllable made Lyssena sad. Would that happen to her as well? Would Erevos stay alone after she was gone?

"I asked her to come with me," he continued. "To leave the human world behind."

Lyssena's fingers curled slightly against the table.

"To The Void?"

"Yes."

She hesitated only briefly before asking, "Why not remain there with her?"

Rolam's expression changed as though the question itself revealed her limited understanding. "In the human realm, there is time. It moves and consumes. It reduces all things."

"In The Void, there is no time. No decay, no aging. She would have remained exactly as she was the day she stepped across the threshold."

Lyssena's breath stilled. *Eternity.*

Eternity was not poetry; it was literal. No aging. No death. No end.

Her mind struggled to wrap around it, because the human part of her measured life in seasons and years and birthdays. But here . . . here those measures dissolved.

She looked back at Rolam.

"And she refused?" she asked.

"She told me," he said, "that her life was meaningful because it ended."

Lyssena swallowed. "And you?" she asked, her voice quieter now. "What did you want?"

"I wanted her," Rolam said simply.

The honesty of it made the air feel tight, even through the mask of a songbird.

Lyssena opened her mouth to ask another question, but the cavern trembled. The shadows along the walls shifted suddenly, pulling inward as though drawn by a force. The glass jars behind Rolam rattled, liquid inside them quivering. And then the entrance of the shop darkened. Rolam's gaze lifted toward the threshold before Lyssena even turned.

The shadows did not merely part. They recoiled.

And in the doorway stood Erevos.

His height seemed greater, where the ceiling dipped lower than their home cavern, his thorns nearly grazing the arch of carved stone, his body outlined in a darkness deeper than the shadows surrounding him. For one suspended moment, everything was still. His gaze found her first, and Lyssena had exactly one second of shame before it moved.

To Rolam.

Erevos growled loudly, the shelves shuddered as the vibration tore through the cavern, glass vessels rattling violently before several toppled from their perches and shattered against the floor in violent bursts of liquid and bone. The scent of brine and decay exploded into the air.

Before Lyssena could speak, Erevos's shadows struck. They did not glide like they did before. They lunged.

Black tendrils shot across the space, coiling around Rolam's torso and arms with brutal force, slamming him backward into the stone wall behind the long table. More glass crashed to the ground, velvet cases overturning, pearls scattering like pale drops of frozen light across the dark floor.

"Erevos!" Lyssena screamed.

The sound tore from her throat as she rushed forward. She nearly slipped on shattered glass, catching herself on the edge of the table as more of Rolam's collected treasures splintered under the assault.

"Stop! Stop—please!" she cried, her hands reaching toward the writhing mass of shadow binding Rolam. "I am alright! He has done nothing!"

Erevos stepped fully into the shop, and his shadows tightened. Rolam did not cry out, but the stone behind him cracked under the pressure.

Erevos opened his mouth. Rows of jagged, shard-like teeth caught what little violet light remained in the cavern.

"Lyssena," he said, his voice no longer restrained, but edged with something feral and ancient, "is mine."

Lyssena's heart slammed violently against her ribs. Rolam had been kind. He had spoken gently. He had shown her beauty. And now he was pinned against the stone because of her.

"Please," she said again, forcing herself forward despite the violent thrashing of shadows, despite the sharp scent of broken glass and spilled preservation liquid burning in her lungs. "Erevos, look at me."

He did not.

The shadows continued to constrict. Lyssena swallowed hard, and she turned her focus not to him, but to the darkness itself. The shadows were alive; they listened to her today and before. They had always listened.

"Leave him," she said, her voice shaking but clear. "He is not a threat."

For one suspended second, nothing happened. But then the shadows faltered. Not fully, but enough. They loosened slightly around Rolam, and Erevos stilled.

The cavern went unnaturally quiet, broken only by the slow drip of liquid from shattered glass and the faint clatter of a pearl rolling to a stop against stone.

Erevos turned his head slowly toward her. "Did you choose him?" he asked.

"No," she answered immediately, stepping closer to him despite the lingering cold radiating from his body. "No, Erevos."

She reached for him. Her fingers slid into his enormous hand, she laced her fingers between his claws and tugged gently, calming him with the only thing she had.

The shadows around Rolam dissolved completely. He slid down the cracked stone wall but remained upright, steady, though shards of glass surrounded him like fallen stars.

Slowly, heat began to return to Erevos's skin, and he stepped closer to her.

His free hand lifted, and he traced his fingers over the smooth curve of her masked head, down along the line where her shoulder started.

Lyssena exhaled shakily. "He was telling me a story," she murmured.

She turned her head toward Rolam. He had not moved to attack. He had not spoken in protest. Instead, he was staring at the broken remnants of his collection scattered across the floor. After a moment, he lifted his gaze to her.

"I have been collecting these," Rolam said, though his voice had grown quieter, "for a very long time."

His eyes drifted briefly to a cracked glass vessel leaking liquid across shadow. "My human liked to collect objects from every place we traveled. Small things. Meaningless to most."

Lyssena felt something twist in her chest. He had recreated that ritual for centuries. "I am sorry," she said, looking at the broken items. "I did not mean for—"

"Why did you decide to live forever?"

The question struck her off guard. Her fingers tightened unconsciously around Erevos's hand. "I—" She faltered, her thoughts scrambling. "If I return to my human home, I will age."

Was she saying those words to feel the comfort of choosing? She had chosen to go with Erevos the day they met. Though now, after everything that happened, she felt the need to state that she still had the choice. She knew Erevos wouldn't kill her or harm her in any way.

"You speak as though that option still exists," he said.

Lyssena blinked. "What do you mean?"

Lyssena turned slowly toward Erevos. He had gone still again, that distant, unreachable quiet he sometimes slipped into, where his gaze aligned with her yet did not seem to land upon. It was as though he were looking through her.

He did that sometimes, and she had never understood why.

"Erevos?" she asked. Her fingers tightened around his hand, seeking reassurance.

"I could not shape matter and shadow as Erevos can," Rolam said from across the fractured shop.

Lyssena's brows drew together immediately. The words felt disconnected from her question, and she was losing patience. "*What* do you mean?" she asked again.

Rolam's gaze did not waver.

"You ate my shadows, Lyssena," Erevos said before Rolam could say a word. His voice was no longer feral. "You are part of me."

Lyssena felt her stomach drop, a hollow plunge beneath her ribs that left her lightheaded.

"You ate my shadows."

The words replayed in her mind, rearranging themselves into a meaning she did not want to assemble. Everything she consumed in The Void had been crafted. All of it . . .

Her mouth went dry. Everything I ate was . . . Him.

She was surrounded by demons.

One of them was Erevos. The one she had trusted most.

"You lied to me."

Chapter Forty-Three

The Last Choice

Erevos

"You said you wanted me to choose you in return," Lyssena said, and Erevos felt her anger. Hot, bubbling anger that spread through her. Unintentionally, as she was wearing his shadows, he consumed every single drop of it.

His spikes reacted; they burned like fire as they grew heavier. Erevos growled and took a step back. He did not understand what was happening to him, what was the reason for an emotion to make him feel pain.

"Lyssen—"

"I believed you. I believed you saved me and wished me well," she said, clenching her fists.

"I hav—"

"You have *not!*"

Torturous pain crawled along his spine; his spikes felt even heavier than before. "You deserve to hear it from me," Erevos said at last, ignoring the agony his body was going through. He wanted his songbird to understand. He did not betray her; he never lied.

Erevos was clueless himself.

"I felt you change the first time you consumed the bread I shaped from my shadows."

His gaze did not leave her face. "It was not visible. Not in any way your human senses would detect. But the darkness did." His jaw tightened. "It leaned toward you. It recognized something within you that had not existed before."

A pause followed, and Lyssena took a step back.

"I did not know it would affect you," he said, and he wished for his songbird to be closer.

"At first, I did not even understand why you felt . . . different. I stood in the cave and watched you. I listened to the cadence of your breathing. I measured the rhythm of your pulse. And yet there was something threaded through you, something that had not been there the day before."

His shadows stirred faintly at his feet. "It took time to assemble the pieces. To recall the exact moment the bread dissolved against your tongue. To remember the pull I felt in my own shadows when you swallowed." His eyes darkened further. "They answered you."

Erevos's greatest desire was for Lyssena to choose him back. He asked when they first spoke, and he wanted to ask again.

"Because I was uncertain, I created the oxygen mask. I told myself it was a precaution. The Void was not built for lungs such as yours. I would not risk your life on an assumption."

He learned he could shape and refine his own shadows the day he understood what it was he truly consumed. It was *devotion.*

The temple in Lyssena's village—where humans gathered daily to kneel, to bow their heads, to whisper desperate prayers toward gods who had never existed—had been a feast laid unknowingly at his feet. Their belief soaked into stone and timber, and he drank it through the cracks in the foundation.

So he carved a chamber of shadow beneath the altar, a room no human eyes could fully perceive, and allowed small "miracles" to manifest in answer to their prayers. A healed wound, a whispered omen, a flicker of divine presence in the dark. They wept, and they worshipped harder. They fed him.

For centuries, devotion poured into him like wine into an endless chalice, and he grew vast on it, stronger. He became the dark beneath the altar. The shadow in the silence. The unseen chamber behind the statues of gods sculpted to nothing at all.

That power allowed him to bend particles, to coax matter into new arrangements, to weave shadow with substance until it resembled bread warm from a human oven. That power allowed him to create sustenance from himself. And, apparently, that power allowed him to change her.

"I did not intend to alter you, Lyssena," he said. "But when you consumed what was mine . . . You consumed me."

When Lyssena heard the truth in his voice, Erevos felt her anger turn into something he did not know how to name. It did not burn, yet it was no relief either.

"If you lie to me now, then I shall be dead."

And with those words, she removed the mask before Erevos could reach her.

The songbird's porcelain face lifted away from her skin, and for a suspended moment, the cavern seemed to inhale.

If Erevos had a heart, it would have stopped at that exact moment.

Her long brown hair spilled over her shoulders in a silken cascade. It slid over her collarbones, over the rise of her chest, strands clinging to her lips where her breath had warmed them. Her green eyes lifted to meet his.

He could feel the rapid flutter of her pulse at her throat, the slight tremor in her fingers where they curled around the discarded mask. She was afraid.

And she was choosing to stand before him anyway.

Erevos did not move, but every shadow in the cavern leaned toward her.

For a long moment, Lyssena said nothing. Her fingers tightened around the mask still hanging at her side.

With no oxygen, a human would have died by now, of that Erevos was certain. Though she did not move at all, and in the first few moments, she did not even breathe.

"You should have told me."

Erevos felt warm again. Hearing her voice, not muffled by the songbird's head.

"You should have trusted me enough to let me decide what to do with that truth."

Erevos inclined his head. "Yes."

There was no defense.

Her throat moved as she swallowed. "You took something from me. Even if you did not mean to." Her eyes shone now, not weak, not small, but bright with emotion. "You took the option of death. You took the illusion that I was still untouched by this world."

The shadows recoiled faintly at the strain in her voice.

"But," she continued, and that single word altered the space between them, "you also saved my life."

Erevos stilled.

"You saved me the night you found me. You fed me when I would have starved. You sheltered me when I was terrified. You answered questions you did not understand simply because I asked them."

Erevos took a step toward her.

"You learned for me, Erevos. You did not know how to speak gently, so you tried. You did not know what comfort was

—so you studied it. You did not understand humans—and yet you listened."

Each word settled into him.

"You created air for me because you were afraid I would die." Her lips trembled. "You built spaces I could sit in. You watched the way I reacted to things and adjusted. You have never once forced me to kneel. Never once demanded obedience."

"You wanted me to choose you."

He did. That was his greatest desire.

"And I am angry," she admitted. "I am angry that the choice feels smaller than it did before. I am angry that the path back to my village no longer exists in the way I believed it did."

Her hand rose slowly, pressing against her own chest. "But you did not do this to trap me. You did not feed me your shadows with the intention of stealing my future. You did it because you did not yet understand the consequences of loving something fragile."

Loving.

Erevos felt something inside him fracture quietly.

"I was a girl in that village," she continued. "I would have married. Been beaten and enslaved. Grown old beneath the same roof where I was born. I would have believed the world ended at the edge of those fields."

Her lips curved. "You showed me it does not."

She stepped closer to him.

"You taught me that fear can be faced. That darkness is not always cruelty. That power does not have to mean harm."

Her fingers lifted slowly and pressed against the center of his chest, where shadows coiled beneath the surface of him. "You helped me become more than I would have ever been allowed to be there."

His chest burned so much he was afraid he would harm his songbird's hand.

"Do I wish you had told me sooner?" she asked.

"Yes."

A tear slipped down her cheek, though she did not look away.

"But do I believe you meant to steal my will?"

She shook her head.

Erevos lowered himself then, their eyes aligned without her needing to tilt her chin upward.

"I am sorry," he said. "I would undo the harm if I could." His massive hand hovered near her waist but did not touch.

"If you walk away from me now, I will not stop you."

The shadows trembled at the lie his nature wanted to tell, that he would drag the world down before he let her go.

"I will endure it," he finished quietly.

"I choose you, Erevos."

And with those words, he knelt, and both of them leaned against each other, completely forgetting about Rolam.

Epilogue

In the seasons that followed in the human world, The Void changed as well.

Not in structure, its endless dark still stretched vast and ancient, but in texture.

Where once there had been only shadowed stone and silent rivers of black current, there were now color and softness woven into one specific home. Cushions in deep sapphire and burnished gold lay scattered across the shadow home. Blankets of crimson and emerald were folded over the backs of shadow-shaped chairs. Pillows embroidered in beautiful patterns rested against walls that had never before known ornament.

Lyssena had arrived one afternoon with a list.

It had been long. *Very* long.

Erevos had taken the parchment from her hands and stared at it as though it were a battle strategy. Rolam, standing beside him, had leaned in with mild curiosity.

"Humans require this much . . . padding?" Rolam had asked.

"Yes," Lyssena had replied firmly. "And more."

She was holding her belly, caressing it gently.

And so the two demons had gone to the human realm together, a sight that would have shattered fragile mortal minds, slipping through markets and coastal towns, returning hours later with bundles of fabric, lanterns with stained glass panels, and an alarming number of decorative pillows.

The Void had never looked the same again.

Lyssena's gowns changed as well.

Each of her gowns was adorned with delicate strands of pearls stitched along hems and sleeves.

Rolam had supplied many of them, and Erevos had said nothing.

But the next time Lyssena asked for pearls, they had appeared in quantities that rivaled any collection Rolam had ever assembled.

She hosted tea parties.

In The Void.

A round table now stood in one of the broader rooms, draped in layered fabrics and surrounded by mismatched chairs that had once belonged to human kitchens and seaside porches. Porcelain cups rested upon delicate saucers, and steam curled upward from fragrant tea.

Lyssena was the only one who drank it.

Erevos sat with ancient dignity, a massive clawed hand wrapped carefully around a cup far too small for him, though he never lifted it to his lips. Rolam, ever adaptable, occasionally mimicked the gesture purely for her amusement.

They discussed absurd things, fabric patterns, and human customs. The merits of colored lanterns versus silver ones.

The Void listened.

And then there were the nights.

The cave that had once felt unbearably vast now often echoed with breathless moans and the sound of shadow hitting skin.

They fucked like rabbits.

Hands, mouths, shadows—nothing about them was timid. The darkness coiled and uncoiled in response to her pleasure, the cavern walls warming when her voice rose and fractured.

One evening, draped in a pearl-threaded gown that clung to her body, she wandered the home alone while Erevos lingered in a distant chamber. She paused beside one of the smooth shadow-walls, tilting her head thoughtfully.

"If you are everything here," she murmured to the wall, "then you can feel this."

And slowly, she traced the flat of her tongue along the cool surface.

From the far end of their home, Erevos appeared at the threshold moments later, shadows snapping violently at his heels, his composure obliterated and his body betraying him entirely.

Lyssena smiled.

She never questioned again whether their home was part of him. She simply used the knowledge to her advantage.

Later still, beneath softer light and quieter breath, she fastened something around his wrist. A simple braided bracelet woven from dark thread and threaded with a single small pearl.

"I want us to match," she had said.

Erevos had stared at the delicate thing as though it were a relic forged by gods. He extended his hand without hesitation and saw she wore one too.

And though he remained vast and ancient and terrible to behold, there were now moments where the most powerful demon in The Void could be found seated beside a human woman in pearls, wearing a small bracelet, listening intently as she explained why emerald cushions were superior to gold.

And in the deepest chamber, beneath colored lantern light and silk-draped stone, Lyssena sat beside Erevos.

Forever, with three pearl bracelets—one of them was small.

About the Author

Nicole A. Sterling writes dark and spicy fantasy full of feral women and obsessive monsters. She believes rage is sacred, love should be all-consuming, and happy endings should still leave bruises.

When she's not summoning demons, she runs a business and tells plot twists to her dog.

Ethereal Ties: The Rose and the Guardian is her debut novel, the first in a series where women don't want equality, they want revenge.

Rolam's happy ending is to come.

Acknowledgments

Writing a second book feels very different from writing the first. The first was written with hope, and the second was written knowing someone is waiting.

To my family and friends, thank you for standing beside me not only when the words flowed easily, but especially when they didn't. Thank you for listening to half-formed plot ideas, for tolerating my distracted stares into nothingness, for understanding when I disappeared into fictional worlds for hours at a time. Your support has never felt small to me. It is deeply cherished.

To my readers, my dear, patient readers, thank you. There is something surreal about knowing that the worlds I build are received with excitement on the other side. Your messages, your theories, your love for these characters... it changes the experience of writing in the most beautiful way. It makes the long nights feel shared. It makes the risks feel worth taking.

Knowing you were waiting for this story gave it weight. It gave it *shadows*.

I am endlessly grateful that you choose my books, my monsters, and my love stories.

And I hope you will continue choosing them.

Forever.

For more about Nicole A. Sterling

Want more dark fantasy, obsessive monsters, and unhinged women? Let's connect:

Instagram: @nicoleasterling
TikTok: @nicoleasterling1
Website: www.nicoleasterling.com
Goodreads: Nicole A. Sterling
Facebook Group: Nicole A. Sterling's Monster Lair
Patreon: Nicole A. Sterling
Amazon: Nicole A. Sterling

Join the author's Patreon for more exclusive content.
patreon.com/cw/NicoleASterling

Also by Nicole A. Sterling

Ethereal Ties Series
The Rose and the Guardian
The Peony and the Guardian
More titles in the series coming soon.

Earthly Ties Series
The Warden and the Warrior
More titles in the series coming soon.

A Godless World Duology
A Prayer to No God
A Sin to A Demon